Georgiana M. Craik

Only a butterfly and other stories

Georgiana M. Craik

Only a butterfly and other stories

ISBN/EAN: 9783742809858

Manufactured in Europe, USA, Canada, Australia, Japa

Cover: Foto ©Andreas Hilbeck / pixelio.de

Manufactured and distributed by brebook publishing software
(www.brebook.com)

Georgiana M. Craik

Only a butterfly and other stories

CONTENTS.

ONLY A BUTTERFLY.

ONLY A BUTTERFLY.

CHAPTER I.

HILDA FORD was one of the people whom one always likens to an April day—a creature half child, half woman; impetuous, passionate, loving, changeful; whom you never expect to be wise, or rational, or useful, or consistent, but only to charm you like some wild sweet flower. Women of this sort make histories for themselves: they cannot live quietly or dully: out of the tamest environment they evolve a temporary romance: there is no abiding grey sky for them, but only alternating cloud and sunshine; and their joys are keen and their sorrows generally pass away. Upon the whole, I think the world treats them kindly: they give their light to it, and it, on its side, in their passage through it, breaks but few of the bright feathers of their plumage.

Hilda's life, until she was seventeen, had been uneventful enough. She had lost her father and mother when she was a mere child, and since their death she had lived in the school of a Miss Fielding, where she had been placed, and very happily, by the only near relation whom she had in the world—a half brother, a dozen years older than herself. He was a soldier, and had been for the last six years with his regiment in India. In a year more, when Hilda should be eighteen, he expected to come home on furlough, and to take his sister to live with him. But in the mean time Hilda was seventeen and not eighteen, and Miss Fielding's school was about to be broken up on account of her marriage, and Hilda, being considered too old to go to a fresh school elsewhere, for this year to come was to be sent to the house of her godmother, a Mrs. Erle, who lived in Lancashire.

Mrs. Erle had been asked to receive her, and had consented, a little (or so, at least, she said) to Hilda's dismay. "For it will be so dull that I don't know what will become of me," she protested. "I shall have nothing to do but to sit demurely in a high-backed chair, and knit stockings, I suppose, and talk about the last century. I don't think that in that house they talk about anything more modern than the last century, and the time when George the Third was king."

Hilda had been commiserating her own fate in speeches of this sort for some weeks past; she was a young person, you see, without much reverence for antiquity.

It was breaking-up day at Miss Fielding's—the day

of final breaking up, after which the school was to exist no longer. It had been a large school, and some of the girls—perhaps the greater number of them—cared very little for the fact that they were never to meet together any more. But some few of them cared, and amongst these few, and even foremost amongst them, was Hilda Ford, for Hilda, as I have said, was of a passionate nature, and felt most things that happened to her for the moment very keenly. She loved Miss Fielding in an eager, impetuous, childish way. She had lived with her so long, that she had ceased to regard her as a schoolmistress, and had long been in the habit of clinging to her, and petting her, and hanging about her in a manner that astonished the other girls. But Miss Fielding, I think, liked to be hung about and petted, and cared more, I suspect, for this one troublesome little gipsy—who treated her as if she were flesh and blood, and not a mere embodiment of rules and authority—than she did for all the remaining members of her flock.

Hilda had spent the greater part of this breaking-up morning in dexterously threading her way through the confusion of the house, flinging off embraces and farewells at every turn, and coolly counting them up as she dispensed them on her fingers. "I only missed two girls out of the whole twenty-eight," she quietly boasted afterwards. Her schoolfellows and Hilda had got on well together up to a certain point; but ardent schoolgirl friendships were not things to which Hilda was naturally very much addicted. She reserved her enthusiasm for other creatures than those of her own species. Here at school she had reserved the whole of her enthusiasm for Miss Fielding, and it was only to Miss Fielding that she showed any emotion before she went away.

She had gone through all the ceremonies of leave-taking with the girls dry-eyed, flitting from one to another as lightly and soullessly as a bird; but when the fly that was to take her to the station was in readiness she went to her friend's room, and entered silently, and closed the door behind her, and then all at once threw herself upon Miss Fielding's neck, and burst into a fit of tears. For two or three minutes she sobbed as if her heart would break.

"I can't bear it! I don't how to bear it! I wish I could die when I go away from you!" she sobbed.

"You foolish child!" Miss Fielding said; but after she had said that she took the girl into her arms, and held her on her bosom without another word.

So Hilda sobbed for two or three minutes, and then looked up, panting and penitent.

"I knew I—I should do it: it—it has been coming on all the morning," she said deprecatingly.

"Well—and now is it over?"

"I don't know; I h-hope it is. You are not angry, are you?"

"Not particularly."

"I will try to be good again now—I will, indeed.
I have been very good all the morning, till—till
now."

"Yes, because you have had little to try you. You
have been very good till now, and you will be very
good again in an hour, and by this evening you will
be quite restored to happiness—you foolish, changeful
child!"

"*You* need not call me changeful. I have never
changed in my love for you."

"No, you have never changed in that." And then
Miss Fielding kissed the girl again. "God bless you!
We shall never forget one another. Now go, my
darling," she said. And Hilda went, swallowing down
her tears, softly closing the door of the little well-
known parlour behind her, and then darting like the
wind along the passages to the entrance hall, lest any
one should meet her and see her face.

"Well, there is an end of it! And now I wish the
whole house was pulled down to the ground, and that
Miss Fielding's parlour hadn't two bricks of it left
upon one another!" she astonished the respectable
staid servant who accompanied her to the railway by
exclaiming as the fly turned from the door.

"Miss Hilda!" ejaculated the good woman, who
had seen very various demonstrations of emotion from
the young ladies who on many breaking-up days had

taken their departure from Miss Fielding's, but never one like this.

Hilda, however, was not in a mood to relish being wondered at.

"You sit and stare at me as if I had come out of a lunatic asylum, Bates. Well, I've been crying! Do you think I can't tell that you know that?"

"I'm very sorry, Miss Hilda," Bates recommenced (and she was thinking to herself, 'There must have been a wonderful blow up with missis just at the end!'), but Hilda snapped at her before she could proceed further.

"What should you be sorry about? Did you think I was to go away from her singing and dancing, when I care for her more—more than I care about anybody else in the world?"

Her voice shook, and she gave one great fresh sob.

"Don't you now, Miss Hilda—now, don't you, dear!" Bates ejaculated hurriedly.

"Don't what?" And Hilda stared steadily into Bates's face, with the tears running down her cheeks.

"Don't you cry. Isn't she going to be married? and won't you both be as happy presently as the day is long?"

"*I* am not going to marry her, Bates?"

"Lord bless you! I should hope not, Miss."

"Then why should you say I'm going to be happy?

I'm not going to be happy. Do you know where I'm going?"

"Into Lancashire, isn't it, Miss?"

"Yes—to a great smoky town, where I shall get all dried up, like a haddock or a red herring."

"I hope not, Miss Hilda."

"I shall, though. What is the good of hoping that a thing won't be when you know it will? That's childish. Did you ever hear of mummies, Bates?"

"What, dead people, Miss?"

"Yes, dead people who are dried up so hard, that they last for ever."

"Lor! I don't see the good of that, Miss Hilda."

"Not of lasting for ever? Well, it's a matter of taste. Bates, I wonder if I shall ever see you again?"

"I hope so, Miss. Eh, dear me, why shouldn't you?"

"Oh, there's no reason against it that I know of, except that the world is rather a big place. So, in case I shouldn't, I think—Bates, I think I'll kiss you."

"Bless your heart, dear, you never was like some of the young ladies, who hadn't a civil word or look to give one."

"Wasn't I? Well, I had faults of some other kind, I suppose. Oh, Bates, I'm sick at heart. I never was so miserable in all the course of my life. There, we have got to the station—and it's a mercy, or I should have done something odd. Get out, Bates, and don't

put on a face like that. Look merry, like me. One
would think it was *you* who were going to be made
into a mummy."

"'Pon my word, ma'am, I was glad to get her safe
in the railway carriage, and see the guard a locking
the door," Bates gravely protested afterwards, in de-
livering her report to Miss Fielding. "I never yet see
a young lady take on so, and just in half-a-dozen
moods a minute. Why, ma'am, she hugged me round
the neck when I was a leaving her, as if it might have
been yourself."

"It is the last little shred of the old life," Hilda
thought to herself. "Now it is all at an end, every bit
of it." And she gathered herself into the corner of
the carriage, and quietly let her tears begin to rise.
She had insisted on taking possession of an empty
carriage. "I'll cry till I am tired, and then have done
with it. I am a great fool, I know that," she said.
So she cried off and on for half an hour, and at the
end of that half hour, raising her head, she began to
notice how pretty the bright green country was around
her, and to find that it was possible to take a little
interest in it; and then the train stopped at a station,
and two travellers entered her carriage, and she felt
ashamed at the thought that her eyes must be red,
and, vexed with herself, vowed suddenly that she would
not shed another tear: so she looked at the prospect
with greater earnestness, and set herself to watch the

winding rivers and the swelling hills, and the sweet
English villages lying amongst their trees, till presently
her lips fell to breaking into little smiles of pleasure;
and then, as the soft south faded back further and
further into the distance behind her, and the north
with its bleaker hills and greyer landscape began to en-
compass her, her thoughts too slowly left the south, and
began to stretch forward to the future, and to her new
home. And when at last the train stopped at the final
station, and some one coming to the carriage-door said,
inquiringly, "Miss Ford?" curiosity and speculation
were far more lively feelings in her than misery, as
she started from her seat and answered, "Yes."

It was Mrs. Erle's son who had come to meet her,
and in a few minutes more she was driving by his
side, in the twilight, through the lighted streets.

CHAPTER II.

It was a short drive and a silent one. Hilda said little; Mr. Erle still less. He had received her kindly, but conversation within a cab that is rolling over stony streets is a thing not to be kept up without difficulty, and Mr. Erle seemed indisposed to attempt it. So they drove side by side, with the interchange of very few words, till at the end of a quarter of an hour their journey ended before the door of a dull enough looking brick house.

The house was dull on the outside, and the parlour, in which a quarter of an hour later Hilda found herself seated at her first meal, was, to tell the truth, dingy and dull enough too. It was summer time, so, though a lamp was burning — for the evening had closed in—there was no fire, and the lamp-light fell cheerlessly on drab-coloured curtains and horsehair-covered chairs, and on Mrs. Erle's black widow's dress. Mrs. Erle was a quiet, anxious-looking woman, with a plain, kind manner, and rather a plaintive voice.

"We must try to make you happy with us; but you will find us very quiet, my dear—very quiet," she said to Hilda, as the girl was taking off her travelling things: and Hilda shivered a little, I am afraid, as she tried to make some civil answer. "It will be frightfully dull, I am afraid," she was thinking to herself. "I never was in such an ugly house in my life; and Mr. Erle doesn't seem to have the power of opening his lips."

But, if Mr. Erle was unnecessarily silent, Mrs. Erle, when they had taken their seats around the table, did her best to talk to the girl. She had been an old friend of Hilda's mother, and she had not seen Hilda for ten years, and she had many things to ask her. It was all strange old-world talk to Hilda—of people who were dead, and times that were gone, and states of existence that had passed away almost before she had come into life at all; but, such as it was, it kept them from silence. "And, indeed," as Hilda wrote afterwards to Miss Fielding, "we might almost have been comfortable, if all the time we were talking Mr. Erle had not put me in mind of the skeleton at an Egyptian feast. He sat at one end of the table and carved the chicken, and hardly ever uttered a word. I don't think—do you?—that people have any right to sit with others like skeletons. I am sure, when tea was over and he went away, I was quite glad to see the door shut behind him."

Mr. Erle had risen up when their meal ended.

"You are not going to work any more to-night, are you, Michael?" his mother said to him as he was leaving the room; but he merely made a murmured answer—the purport of which Hilda, at any rate, could not understand, if his mother did—as he opened the door.

"I am always trying to keep him from doing work late at night: it is so very bad for him," Mrs. Erle said in her plaintive voice when he had gone.

"Is it?" asked Hilda, indifferently.

"Oh yes, my dear, very bad—very bad," Mrs. Erle said, with a sigh. And then they sat down upon the sofa and resumed their talk.

"What in the world shall I do with myself here, I wonder, all day long?" Hilda said to herself next morning as she dressed.

She had gone early to bed, for she had been tired with her journey, and had slept well; and now a new day had come—a dull, grey day; and as she drew up the blind in her room, and looked out across the street towards the opposite row of grim monotonous houses, she asked herself this question rather dolefully.

"What in the world shall I do? Nothing but brick walls out-of-doors, and nothing indoors but such a dreary pair of people! Oh dear, how shall I bear it for a whole long year?"

"You never lived in a town before, did you, Hilda?" Mrs. Erle asked her presently. "Ah, yes, it is a great change from the country, and you will feel

the confinement at first, I dare say; but we are very
healthy here; we have always found the situation
particularly healthy, and it's nice and open at the
back. We really have some quite pretty walks. I
am not very much of a walker myself, and Michael is
so much engaged; but if we could find some young
companion for you, you might go out together, and
it would be very pleasant; only, I am sorry to say, I
know so few young people. I am sure I wish the
house was likely to be a little livelier for you, dear
child! But you must just try and make the best of
us, you know." And she put her hand on the girl's
shoulder, and patted it; and Hilda said, "Oh yes,"
and tried to think of something else to say that should
be both truthful and polite, but could not, and so
turned away and held her tongue, and stood at one
of the parlour windows, looking out.

They had already had breakfast, and Mr. Erle had
left them and gone up to his study. Mr. Erle had
exchanged a few sentences with Hilda in the course
of the half hour that they had sat together at table:
Mrs. Erle had talked a good deal in her gentle in-
effective way. Her talk was a thing that was much
like softly trickling water, that went on without cessation, quietly, monotously, drowsily. I think there was
something rather soothing about it to those who were
not young, and had sympathy with quiet things. But
Hilda had not much sympathy with quiet things, and

so it wearied her. She stood at the window, leaning her forehead rather hopelessly against the glass. "I wish I was at school again! I wish I was in the schoolroom, with all the buzz of the girls' voices round me," she was thinking.

Mrs. Erle was pottering about the room, setting this thing and that in order. It was a fair sized room, and they seemed to use it as a general living room, and both to sit and eat there. It had a well-worn horsehair sofa in it, and a dozen upright-backed chairs, and one armchair that stood by the fireside. There was an old-fashioned dim-faced glass above the chimney-piece, and a square table in the middle of the floor, and a spider-legged sideboard, dark with age, and in one corner a little bookcase filled with books.

"We have so many books in the house, but I like to keep them out of this room," Mrs. Erle had told Hilda. "They make such a terrible litter in a place. I am always trying to keep Michael's room in order; but it is no use: I can't do it. He sets everything down anywhere, and you have no sooner got it a little straight than he turns it all topsy-turvy again. He always puts me in mind of a sick man in a new-made bed—for it goes to my heart to see the way men pull the clothes this way and that; so that you've not laid them smooth and nice for five minutes before they're looking again as if they were lying in a

ploughed field. I am fond of seeing things neat and
straight myself; but I dare say, like most young
people, you will think it an old-fashioned taste, my
dear."

Hilda had got a bit of crochet in her hand, which
she was twisting round and round as she stood looking out into the street. She had no other work except that to do: she stood yawning and wondering
how the morning was to pass.

"I shall have to leave you for a little while to
amuse yourself," Mrs. Erle said to her presently. "I
have always my house matters to see to in the mornings, you know; but you will find books to read—or,
perhaps, you may have some letters that you want to
write? And then, if the rain holds off—only I am
very much afraid that it is going to be wet—we might
take a little turn before dinner. There is a nice
square garden just round the corner, where I often go
for half an hour. I find it very convenient, because
it is so near—for one likes to get a breath of fresh
air, especially in summer—and I am not a good
walker, I am sorry to say. I never was a very good
walker, even in my young days, and one doesn't improve in that respect as one grows older. But we
will try to get a little turn, at any rate, if we do nothing more."

So then she went away, and Hilda was left alone

—to her crochet, or her letters, or her reading, as she chose.

She went after a while to the bookcase, and began to read the titles of the books. There was Gibbon's Decline and Fall, and Bacon's Works, and Robertson's Charles the Fifth, and the Tatler and Spectator, and a Cyclopædia of general knowledge, filling a whole shelf.

"Dear me, what a collection!" Hilda said to herself.

She took out a volume of the Spectator presently, and sat down with it on one of the straight-backed chairs beside the window. The window had a wire blind before it, and when she sat down the blind was higher than her head, and she could not see out, and this made her cross. Both room and street seemed duller than ever, as she sat with the unopened book upon her knees, looking on the opposite pavement through the blind's blurring medium. "How can people go on living in such a dreary place? Oh dear me, how can Mrs. Erle bear to live here all her life long?" Hilda thought.

It was all so silent: not full of a living silence, as the country is, but heavy and oppressive with a stillness that was dead and leaden. Within the house there was scarcely a sound of any kind; without there were the steps of a few passers-by, a street cry now and then, occasionally a quick passing patter of youthful feet; but these things broke the silence only momentarily.

"I wonder if there are people living in all these other houses?" Hilda thought. "If there are, why don't they come out? Do they all sit, as I am doing, behind wire blinds, and try to read mouldy old books? And oh, I wonder if they are all longing, as I am, to be somewhere else?"

She took her book to the sofa presently, and curled herself into one corner with it and opened it, and began to read a little. It was a curious sort of book, she thought; but when she had once begun she went on reading it, yawning and breaking off sometimes, but always going back to it again, with a sort of feeble interest.

"Ah, you have got a volume of the Spectator? That is very delightful reading—isn't it?" Mrs. Erle said, coming into the room after an hour or two, and speaking quite cheerfully on seeing her guest so well employed. "I am glad you like that kind of book, my dear, for it is so good for young people. There is Rasselas, too: did you ever read Rasselas? It is Dr. Johnson's, you know. 'Rasselas, or the Happy Valley.' It is most charming."

"Is it a story?" asked Hilda, with a gleam of hope.

"Well, it is a sort of story: it is what you may call a story, and something more. I will give it to you presently, for I am sure you would like it. I am quite pleased to see you able to amuse yourself so sensibly, Hilda. I am afraid there are a great many young ladies now who never care to open a rational book — they think of nothing but gaiety and excitement; but I am so glad to see that you can sit down quietly and make yourself happy in this way. It is a great blessing to be able to do it, dear. I always had those kind of tastes myself; and as for Michael, you know you hardly ever see him without a book in his hand. *He* carries it a little too far, indeed: we mustn't let you grow quite into such a bookworm as he is," said Mrs. Erle, smiling gently at her own joke.

"Good gracious, what a horrible idea!" thought Hilda to herself.

The rain began to fall at twelve o'clock, and came down steadily all through the afternoon, so they did not go out even to the square garden. They dined at one, and after dinner Mrs. Erle brought out her knitting, and Hilda did her crochet, and they talked; and then Mrs. Erle produced Rasselas, and Hilda began the perusal of that celebrated book.

"Perhaps just at first you may think the style a little stiff, my dear," Mrs. Erle said to her. "Of course it is very unlike the slip-shod writing we have so much of nowadays; but I hope you won't feel that that is any objection to it. At any rate, I am sure you will enjoy it thoroughly when you have once got into it."

And then, with a comfortable conviction that she had provided excellent entertainment for her guest during the remainder of the afternoon, Mrs. Erle put on her spectacles and began to read her newspaper; and Hilda, book in hand, retired to the sofa again, and I am afraid that during the hour that followed she found the style of Rasselas very stiff indeed.

Would the long day never pass? she thought, and would all days be like this one? She welcomed the sight even of Mr. Erle when he came down at six o'clock to tea, because his coming made some break in the weary monotony of the hours. Before tea time came she had gone upstairs, and had dressed herself in a pretty fresh muslin dress, and had put a bright bow in her hair. The light-coloured muslin and the bright ribbon seemed all out of keeping with the house and her surroundings, but she felt as though she must at least make herself pretty, or she could not bear the pervading gloom.

The rain had ceased, and a gleam of unexpected sunlight fell upon her as she came into the room, and Mrs. Erle looked up at her with lifted eyebrows of sudden surprise. But the surprise after a moment passed into a smile.

"My dear," she said, "you are very like your mother. Do you know, I didn't see it at first. I thought you took most after your father's family, but as you came in just now you looked so like what your mother used to be. That is such a pretty dress, Hilda; only is it not perhaps just a little too nice to have put on when we are all by ourselves?"

"Oh no, not at all," replied Hilda coolly. "I always dress in the evenings, and I like to wear muslins when it is fine."

And then the tea bell rang, and Mr. Erle came down, and he too, as he entered, looked at Hilda.

I think the dingy room was the better for her presence in it. The rain, as I said, had ceased, and the evening had begun to brighten, and the sunlight and her own consciousness of looking well gave a fillip to the girl's drooping spirits. She began to talk to Mrs. Erle with more liveliness than she had yet done. Once or twice, too, as she talked, Mr. Erle laughed at what she said, and Hilda, who loved to hear her sayings listened to, and if she could provoke nothing better than laughter by them, at any rate infinitely preferred that doubtful appreciation of their excellence to no appreciation at all, brightened visibly as he laughed.

You see she was not used to silence or dulness, and she sorely wanted something or some one to play with. She also sorely wanted something to do. "I don't know when I have been a whole day in the house before," she said once, half piteously, as they sat at tea, with a glance towards the window, where the panes were all dry now; but the speech and the glance were lost upon the other two. Mr. Erle calmly buttered a piece of toast while she spoke, and Mrs. Erle merely answered kindly, "Yes, dear, it has been a very dull day to you, I am afraid; but we must hope for better things to-morrow." And then Hilda could say no more, though she thought to herself, "Why need we wait for to-morrow, I wonder! Why in the world should nobody have a walk now, when it is only six o'clock, and the sun won't set for hours?"

But apparently Mrs. Erle was not in the habit of walking after tea; and as for her son—her son was evidently wholly unconscious that any attentions to Hilda were dreamt of from him, for he ate his toast with a perfectly placid face, as though the subject that had been started was one with which he had no conceivable concern, and when tea was ended he went away. Perhaps he had work to do; perhaps Hilda's kittenish presence teased him, and he preferred the silence and safety of his own room.

"She is a pretty little thing, is she not, Michael?" his mother said to him that night, after Hilda had retired to bed; and he looked up at the question from a book he was reading, with a laugh.

"Yes, she is very pretty; but I hardly know what you are to do with her. She will never be content to live our quiet life," he said.

"Do you think she won't?"

"I am afraid she will either upset you in all your usual ways, or else begin to mope and get unhappy.

I suspect we have not been very wise to let her come to us."

"Well, I don't know; I don't feel sure of that."

"We must do our best for her now she is here; but certainly if she tries you too much, the arrangement shall not go on for a whole year. Her brother must find some other place to send her to."

And then Mr. Erle went back to his book. Poor Hilda, softly singing to herself, to keep up her spirits, as she was going to bed, would have got hot, perhaps, if she had heard that talk, and learnt the fact that Mr. Erle intended to make the length of her stay in his house depend upon her good behaviour. She would have got hot if she had known it; but happily she did not know it. Mercifully we are so often ignorant of the things that are said of us behind our backs.

CHAPTER III.

I AM afraid, however, that Mr. Erle's judgment of her was correct enough, and that this poor Hilda was nothing but a foolish child, quite unfitted for leading a sober rational life—a creature who loved excitement, and fretted when she could not get it; who wanted so piteously, just like a kitten, to be amused. How could such a girl be content to sit upon a straight-backed chair, and improve her mind with reading Rasselas? She gave up reading Rasselas very soon, I am sorry to say, and returned to the Spectators, out of which she did contrive to get a little entertainment of a feeble sort; but even the Spectators only pleased her very moderately. She yawned even over Sir Roger de Coverley sometimes. He was amusing enough, but he was too old-fashioned to do more than half entertain her.

A modern novel, of course, would have suited her. She would have curled herself up upon the horsehair sofa, and have been content to read that through the whole length of a summer day; but unhappily Mr. Erle's library was void of modern novels, and one day, when she proposed to go to a circulating library in the town, and bring away from it some of the food for which her soul longed, Mrs. Erle began to cough and look uneasy.

"Well, my dear, I don't know—there is so much rubbish written and printed now," she said hesitatingly. "I don't mean that there is any harm in reading a good novel now and then; but I think, Hilda, if you would read Sir Charles Grandison—you know I offered it to you yesterday—it would be a great deal better for you than these nasty circulating library books. If you will just begin Sir Charles Grandison, you will get amazingly interested in it."

So then with a sigh Hilda, for that day, gave up her projected walk into the town; and an hour afterwards Mrs. Erle found her asleep upon the sofa, with Richardson's famous book open on her knee at its third page.

What was the good of trying to make a sensible woman out of such a child? You might as soon have tried to make the birds in the air turn spinning-wheels instead of singing their useless songs. The turning of spinning-wheels is a more profitable occupation than song-singing; but yet the world has so many people in it who can turn wheels, and saw wood, and draw water. Most of us have to do these things, and are born to do them; perhaps we may leave the few who, like Hilda and the birds, have another kind of vocation given them, to follow that

undisturbed. You could not have made a worker of
this foolish Hilda though you had tried to do it with
all your might. To play with life and look on at
other people's work, and lighten it a little now and
then by throwing some gleams of brightness over it,
that was her business mainly, I believe; to sing, and
make you listen to her; to play, and make you play
too; this was all the use you could put her to, all the
work you could get out of her. If you had made her
sensible, you would have taken away the essence of
her life: she would not have sung to you or played
with you any more.

To such a creature existence was of necessity dull
enough in that quiet house of Mrs. Erle's. What
could she do in it all the day? Like a caged bird,
she began after a very little while to pine and grow
dull and listless. She had no companions—she who
had had troops of companions hitherto nearly all her
life; she had no amusements, and she had got so tired
of trying to amuse herself. Mrs. Erle was very kind
to her; but she did not care for Mrs. Erle. Mr. Erle
sat in his study and did nothing for her. She went
out occasionally, but the town was dull and ugly, and
their walks seldom extended beyond the town. Two
or three times she accompanied Mrs. Erle to the
square garden, and then she refused—a good deal to
Mrs. Erle's distress—to go any more, and persisted in
staying indoors instead of walking. "I don't care

much about square gardens, thank you—I would a
great deal rather stay at home," she said obstinately,
and Mrs. Erle had to go and take her constitutional
by herself.

But yet to stay at home was so very dull too!

"Are you here by yourself?" Mr. Erle said to
her one morning, coming by chance into the sitting-
room in search of a paper that he wanted, and
finding Hilda there all alone, standing by the window,
ignominiously doing nothing.

She would not have let herself be caught standing
so and doing nothing, if she had had any warning of
his coming; but Mr. Erle in his slippers had a way
of moving very noiselessly about the house, and she
had not heard his step until his hand was on the
door. So she coloured, being vexed by his entrance
when she was not expecting him, and then when he
spoke to her—"Yes; Mrs. Erle is out," she answered
shortly.

"And why are you not out too, then?" he asked
next.

"Oh, I don't know. It doesn't seem any good,"
she said rather dejectedly.

"It doesn't seem any good to go out?" He gave
a moment's laugh. "You oughtn't to feel like that."

She made no answer, and he went to a table and
began to turn over some newspapers that were lying
there. For a few minutes they stood back to back.

She was annoyed because she was doing nothing, but yet she would not betake herself to any occupation, lest he should think — which would have been the truth—that it was his presence that had made her occupy herself. She stood looking into the street, thinking in her foolish little heart — "He might do something for me. I am sure he might come at least and talk to me a little," and pouting her rosy lips with an injured, half-pitying feeling as she thought it; he—well, he was turning over his newspapers, and in looking for the thing he wanted in them perhaps he forgot Hilda's existence altogether.

He might have done that for any sign he gave, as two, three, five minutes passed. But at last he seemed to have found what he was in search of, for he selected one paper and threw the rest away, and then, turning round suddenly, he looked again towards Hilda.

He stood still for a moment or two, and after that pause went to her. The poor child looked so lonely in her idleness, that perhaps he was sorry for her. He went to her and said kindly—

"I wish we could do something to make you happier; I am afraid you are often very dull here."

"Oh, it doesn't matter," answered Hilda shortly, but with rather a tremor in her voice.

"Yes, it does matter. I know my mother is very sorry about it," he said.

3*

And then to this there came no answer. There came no answer, but she turned her head away, and after a moment or two—oh, foolish Hilda!—there came an unmistakeable sound of a little childish sob.

Mr. Erle was a shy man, and the colour mounted up into his face; if he could, he would have fled to the farthest attic. He would have done that if he could, only he had not the heart to do it. How could he go away without a word, and leave the child to cry?

And yet what was he to say to her? He might tell her not to cry; but was it likely that she would stop her weeping at his bidding? He could not coax her to stop weeping with sugar-plums, even supposing that he had any sugar-plums in his possession, which was a supposition wide of the truth. What could he possibly say or do that should be kind, and at the same time effectual in stopping what was going on? for she was continuing to cry—that was the serious part of it. Five minutes ago, in spite of her childishness, she had had no more thought of crying than Mr. Erle himself, but yet she was so sorry for her own dreariness that, when in this unexpected way he began to pity her for it too, her own pity joined to his upset her altogether, and she gave one sob, and then another, and then the tears came like an April shower.

"I am very sorry—I am afraid you ought not to

stay here by yourself. My poor child, what can I do for you?" Mr. Erle said, in mingled alarm and distress.

"Oh, never mind. Just—just leave me alone," said Hilda, half inaudibly, with a little gasp.

"But I don't like to leave you alone."

And then Mr. Erle cleared his throat, and gave an uneasy look at the flushed face beside him, and wondered in great perplexity what he should do next.

As for Hilda, she was in a state of entire humiliation, for, like most childish creatures, she could not bear to be thought a child, or to be detected behaving like one, and yet she knew that she was behaving like a child at this moment; and as her sobs ceased the knowledge began to make her very hot and miserable. She wanted to be comforted, and yet she was ashamed of wanting to be comforted. She almost wished that Mr. Erle would go away; and yet if he *had* gone away, in all likelihood she would have burst into tears of even keener self-pity than before.

"I've got nothing to do. I—I shouldn't mind it if I had got something to do," she blurted out faintly and deprecatingly, after a few moments' silence.

"I wonder what we could find for you to do!" Mr. Erle knitted his brows, and began to bite his lips in the vain effort to think of some occupation for her.

"What do you think you would *like* to do?" he said hesitatingly.

"I don't know"—in a tone of deep dejection.

"I am so sorry that we have not got a piano for you yet, but my mother is going to see about hiring one. You would like a piano, would you not?"

"Yes." But the "yes" was uttered very indifferently.

"Would you care to look at any pictures?"

This suggestion came after another pause.

"What sort of pictures?" A humiliating idea flashed through Hilda's mind that he was perhaps going to offer her some little story books with woodcuts in them to amuse her: she turned round to him as she put her question with an angry half-suspicion in her eyes.

"I have a good many engravings. I think, perhaps, you might like to see them."

"Oh!"

"Do you think you would?"

"Ye-es, I might."

"Then I will bring them down. Or—I wonder——" Mr. Erle paused for a moment, and then, with rather an effort, went on quickly—"I wonder if you would rather look at them upstairs?"

"Up in your study?"

"Yes. Will you come with me and see them there?"

"Oh—may I?" For the first time the poor little face began to brighten.

"If you like."

"I think I should like. I get so tired of being alone. I think rooms on the ground floor in a town are so dull." This was said very deprecatingly.

"I am afraid they are. I wish we had a brighter house for you."

"Oh, I suppose I shall get used to it."

With the expectation of a little entertainment before her, Hilda's tone was becoming more hopeful.

"You will certainly find it a little more cheerful upstairs."

"Shall I? I have never been in your study."

"Have you not? I didn't know that."

"But I have wanted to go, because I fancy it must be nice up at the top of the house."

"Very well; come and see if you think it nice."

And so then they went upstairs together. She had stopped her tears, and her elastic spirits were rising; she began to chatter to him as they mounted to his room.

"I think if I had a house in a town I never would live anywhere but at the top of it. It is so nice to get high up, and I shouldn't mind running up and down stairs a bit. I like running up and down stairs.

Oh, what a pretty window!" And with a sudden exclamation of delight she made a childish spring across his room, and began to look out from his open window, laughing with pleasure at the sight of green fields beyond the house-tops, and pale hills far away.

Mr. Erle followed her, and laughed too.

"Yes—I am afraid I have got the best room in the house for myself," he said; "but the arrangement, I suspect, is hardly one that can be changed now. It would not quite suit my mother to have to mount so many stairs up to her sitting-room."

"No, I suppose it wouldn't. But is it not a pity?" asked Hilda innocently. "Does it not seem stupid to have to sit downstairs when it is so nice here? Oh, I like this room; I should never get tired of sitting in it."

"Ahem!" said Mr. Erle—coughing rather unnecessarily.

"What are all those places far away? Look—there is quite a big hill there, with a wood all over it. Oh, what pretty walks there must be there! What is the name of that hill?" asked Hilda.

And then Mr. Erle had to put his head out beside hers and tell her; and having told her the name of one hill, he had to tell her the names of all the other hills, and then to point out the church spires in the town for her, and the various public buildings, and to instruct her in the points of the compass, and show her where, on a clear day, you might see into Westmoreland.

All this took a considerable time to do, and before it was ended the west wind had blown away all traces of Hilda's tears, and she drew her head back into the room blooming and fresh as a rose.

"Shall I give you the pictures now?" asked Mr. Erle.

"Thank you," replied Hilda.

And so Mr. Erle produced a large portfolio, and, having no stand on which to place it, placed it instead between two chairs, and then drew forward another chair for Hilda.

"I think this will do if you sit here. Can you reach them so? Look—place them on that side when you have finished with them. Is that right?"

"Yes," said Hilda, but a little doubtfully.

"You will find that a few of them have no names; but you must ask me anything you want to know."

"Oh yes," said Hilda, very readily.

And then, the next instant, before he had time to turn away—

"Here is one that has no name," she exclaimed quickly.

"That is a very interesting one. It is a John Bel-

lini." Mr. Erle turned back and stood looking over
her shoulder at it.

"Oh!"

The monosyllable came very faintly. To tell the
truth, Hilda had never heard of John Bellini, only
she did not like to say so. The engraving, moreover,
presented no features that appeared interesting to her
.in the least degree. She looked at it blankly for a
few seconds, then, with closed lips, prudently laid it
aside.

"This next is one of Sir Joshua's. You will like
this better."

"Oh yes!"—and Hilda's face began to dimple.
"What a darling little child! What a pretty picture!
Oh yes, I like this ever so much the best," said Hilda
honestly.

"That is very natural. You will find a good many
more Reynoldses here. They are nearly all of them
very beautiful."

And then Mr. Erle made a second movement to
turn away, but Hilda suddenly lifted up her head and
stopped him.

"I once saw a real picture of Sir Joshua
Reynolds'," she said, looking in his face with great
solemnity.

"I dare say," he answered carelessly.

"It was a lady with a little girl in her arms. I
·forget who she was."

"Sir Joshua has painted a good many ladies with little girls in their arms. You will find one or two of them there, I think."

"He was very deaf, wasn't he?"

"Yes, very deaf."

"How horrid is must be to be deaf!"

"*You* wouldn't like it all, I can believe."

"No; I think I would rather die. Just think of never being able to hear what anybody said!"

"You would have to pass your time in reading and meditation, you know."

"Oh, but that would be so dreadful!"

"You oughtn't to think it dreadful to read and meditate."

"No; but to do it all day!"

"That wouldn't suit you, you think?" and then Mr. Erle laughed.

"I don't think it would suit anybody. I think it's so nice to talk, and have people talk to you."

Mr. Erle had been on the point once more of taking his departure, but when Hilda in her childish voice said these last words somehow he had not the heart to go. He remained standing near her for a few minutes longer, dropping out criticisms and remarks as she turned the engravings over, and then, like a man resigning himself to his fate, at last he drew another chair forward and sat down by her side.

She had so many questions to ask him, so many foolish little things to say. He felt as though she were a
child fallen to his charge who would get dull if she
were left to amuse herself, and so he stayed with her
and amused her. He had his day's work to do, but
he thought to himself that he would sit up an hour
or two later, and get it done so. Such an interruption must not occur again; but since it had happened
this once, he would make the best of it. So he
showed his pictures to her, and she chattered to him,
bright and happy as a bird.

The poor child was easily satisfied, you see. She
only wanted a little attention to be paid her, a little
notice to be taken of her, a little kindness to be given
her. No doubt, if it had been Mrs. Erle who had
spent the morning in showing pictures to her, she
would not have looked upon the entertainment so
offered to her as an exciting one at all. She would,
I fear, have yawned over the engravings from the old
masters: she would probably have regarded even the
Sir Joshuas with an indifferent eye. But then she did
not care for Mrs. Erle: she was tired of her; she had
her' with her all day long. She wanted something
new to amuse her, and it was something new to be
talked to by Mr. Erle. Was it not ten times plea-
santer, too, to be sitting up here in this cheerful room
with somebody at her elbow to listen to all she said,
. than to be moping downstairs in the dingy parlour,

with no entertainment but the click of Mrs. Erle's
knitting needles, or the drowsy sound of her monotonous voice?

So she spent her morning chirping over her engravings, and, tame though the amusement might be,
it was the pleasantest morning that she had spent by
a great deal since she had come into the house. Mrs.
Erle, returning home presently and searching for her
in vain downstairs, came up in course of time to the
study, and to her surprise found her truant visitor there.

"Why, Hilda, my dear!" she exclaimed, opening
her eyes at the sight that met them as she opened
the door; and then Hilda turned round with a little
laugh.

"I was so dull downstairs, and Mr. Erle let me
come up here. Isn't it good of him?" she said, and
looked up with an innocent face.

"Ye-es; but you mustn't take up too much of
Michael's time," said his mother dubiously.

"*Am* I taking up your time?" asked Hilda, and
then the round young eyes went wistfully up to his.

What could he do but make a kindly answer to
her? Perhaps he might have been tired of sitting by
her side, of holding the pictures while she looked at
them, of telling her that this was an engraving from
Titian, and this from Gainsborough, and listening to
her crude criticisms and childish questions; but, if he
was, how could he be hard enough to tell her so? He

wanted to go to his work, perhaps; but I think, even before Mrs. Erle came into the room, that he had almost forgiven Hilda for keeping him from his work. When she looked at him with that wistful "*Am* I taking up your time?" could he or any man have made a cruel answer to her?

"You are not taking up more of it than I like you to do," he said.

"Yes, but Michael always works in the mornings, my dear; you must remember that," Mrs. Erle struck in rather uneasily.

"I didn't mean to take him from his work," said Hilda deprecatingly.

"I am sure you did not. It is all quite right, mother. We have nearly reached the end of our pictures," Mr. Erle said quickly.

And then, thinking silence for the moment most prudent, Mrs. Erle went away. But—"It will never do for the child to be sitting there and interrupting him," she thought in a vexed way to herself as she retraced her steps downstairs. "It really is very difficult to know what to do with her. One can't treat her as if she were actually a child, and tell her that she must not do this or that, and yet she wants looking after just as much as if she was ten years old. But, however it is managed, I can't have Michael's time broken in upon. That is the one thing that I will not permit." And Mrs. Erle went down to her parlour, rather

flustered and upset, yet resolute at least—or at any
rate she thought she was resolute—to prevent a repetition of this morning's work.

But it needs an alertness greater than Mrs. Erle's,
and a hand stronger than hers, to hold in the Hildas
and the spoilt children of this world with either bit or
bridle: and so she found. On the day that followed
this first excursion of Hilda to the upper regions of
the house she remained meekly in the parlour, docile
and gentle as a lamb; but on the day that followed
that one, at a time when Mrs. Erle's back was turned,
her errant footsteps softly led her—well, they did not
at first lead her quite so far as up to the study door
again; but this was how it came about:—

There was a staircase window on the upper flight
of stairs—a window from which, though you could
not see so much as from the higher one in Mr. Erle's
room, there were yet pretty glimpses of fields beyond
the town to be caught, and distant hedgerows and
trees. It was a sunny window, too, and on this special morning Hilda said to herself, "I'll go and sit up
there in the sunshine and sew. It is ever so much
nicer to be there than here." So she went up, and
took her work along with her, and sitting down upon
the stairs began to sew and sing.

The house was very quiet, and her voice made a
silvery little twitter in it, like a bird's. Looking up
she could see the door of Mr. Erle's room above her;

eight stairs to mount, and she might have reached it. She raised her eyes, and in her heart she knew that she should like to go up those stairs and tap and ask him to let her in; she was such a child, too, that she almost thought once or twice that she might do it. He would not mind her doing it, she thought; though he was grave, he was always kind to her; he was never cross; she was not afraid of him; she thought if she asked him that he would let her go in and sit and read in that sunny window.

"It wouldn't disturb him a bit, for I could be quite quiet," thought Hilda. "I wonder if I mightn't ask! It is so much nicer in that room than anywhere else." And she went craning her neck again wistfully.

But happily, though she *almost* thought that she might ask Mr. Erle to let her in, some instinct of uncertainty kept her from doing it, and the minutes went by as she sat musing and sewing, and sometimes singing, till more than an hour had passed.

. At the end of that time Mr. Erle's door suddenly opened, and he came out on the landing and began to descend the stairs.

. "I could not think where your voice came from," he said to Hilda as he saw her. "Why, you have been sitting here a long time?"

"Yes, ever so long. Ever since ten o'clock." She said this rather pathetically, but there was a bright, half-expectant look on the little face as it was lifted up. "Did you hear me? I didn't know that you could hear me up there."

"Oh yes, I heard you very well. And, do you know, sometimes I am afraid I may have to ask you not to sing upon the stairs. Shall you mind it if I do?"

"Oh no." But Hilda looked rather crest-fallen.

"I am sorry to have to stop you, but I have to write, you know, and I find it difficult to write with a sound of singing in my ears."

"I never thought of that."

"No, I am sure you did not; and if I were not busy, I should like to hear you sing very much."

"I only did it to amuse myself"—she said this a little dejectedly — "because I have nobody to talk to."

"Poor child! have you no one to talk to? Where is my mother?"

"I don't know," shaking her head.

"Has she gone out?"

"Yes, I think so. Oh yes," suddenly, "I remember: she has gone to Mrs. Coulson's."

"You ought to have gone with her."

"I didn't want to go."

She was still sitting on her stair, and Mr. Erle was standing by her. There was a little pause after that last word, and then he said kindly—

"I wish we had some companions for you, of your

own age. I can understand that all this must be very dreary for you."

"Oh, it can't be helped," said Hilda.

"I am almost afraid it can't, for we lead such a quiet life; but I wish there was something we could do for you."

There was a moment or two's silence, and then Hilda said suddenly—"I liked looking at those engravings the other day."

"Unfortunately, however, I have no more engravings."

"No, I suppose not; but," wistfully, "I wonder if you have anything else?"

"Anything else to show you?"

"Yes."

"Well, I hardly know." A pause. "I am almost afraid I have not."

"You have a great many books?"

"Yes; but you would hardly care for them."

"Not for any of them?"

"I fear not; but," half unwillingly, "you may come and look if you like."

"Oh, may I?" and, without any further invitation, she sprang to her feet.

"I want something below: but you can go up, and I will be with you in a minute or two."

So she went up, and without loss of time began her examination of the book-shelves.

When he joined her, after a little while, he found her gazing at them rather disconsolately.

"I am afraid I can't find anything," she said.

"You will certainly find nothing to suit you on this side of the room," he answered with a laugh. "Whatever chance you have lies in one or other of those two book-cases over there. Come and see if they have anything better to offer you."

He took her to some other shelves, and here she began to brighten again a little; for though there were no books in them exactly such as she desired, still there were various ones that might—in the straits to which she was reduced—be found endurable, she thought. There was Lockhart's Life of Scott, for instance; there was Southey's Life of Nelson; best of all—"Why, there are the Waverley novels; have you read them?" Mr. Erle suddenly asked.

"No. Have you got them?"

"Yes, they are all here."

"Oh, that is delightful!" And the child clapped her hands and laughed with pleasure. "I never thought of you having any novels. Oh, I shall be happy now for ever so long. How could you say that you had no books I should care for? Which one shall I begin with? Which is a good one?"

"Have you never read any of them?"

"Yes, I have read Waverley—that is beautiful, isn't it?—and Ivanhoe."

4*

"Suppose, then, you read Rob Roy; or would you like a very sad one better?"

"I don't know. I think perhaps I should. Is there a sad one that is nice?"

"Yes, the Bride of Lammermoor. There it is."

"I think I will have that, then. Do *you* like it?" suddenly. "Oh, but I suppose you have never read it?" half apologetically.

"Why should you suppose I have never read it?"

"Because I think you wouldn't read novels."

"I don't read many novels now, but I *have* read a good many. I have certainly read all the Waverley novels."

"Oh, I am glad of that!"

"I can't see why you should be glad of it."

"Yes, because it makes you——"

But at this point Hilda, who had begun her sentence quickly, abruptly broke off.

"Because it makes me what?"

"Well—more like other people."

This came out a little unwillingly, and it was followed by a sudden silence. Hilda said nothing more, and Mr. Erle made no answer to her. The conclusion of her speech had been frank, but hardly complimentary perhaps, nor of a nature exactly to induce a reply from him. He took the book that she was going to read down from the shelf, and dusted it while they stood without speaking, then—

"I am glad there are so many Waverley novels to keep you from starvation for a little while," he said with a laugh. "Perhaps by the time you have come to the end of them, we shall be able to find something else for you."

"Thank you," said Hilda demurely, and took her volume.

And then after that she ought to have gone downstairs; but in the first place she was conscious that she had said something which she had better not have said, and in the second place she did not want to go. So she stood for a moment or two hesitating, and then all at once she raised her young childish face to him, and—

"I didn't mean to be rude just now, but I am afraid I was," she exclaimed. "You won't mind it, will you? You won't be angry?"

"Angry?" He laughed at her. "Most certainly not."

"Because you know I didn't mean—"

But Hilda was very doubtful as to what it was that she had not meant, so this sentence, though it was begun energetically, became interrupted after its commencement, and ceased suddenly. As for Mr. Erle, he probably thought that he had heard enough, for he made rather a hasty movement towards his writing-table.

"I hope you will like your book. I am very glad

we have found it for you," he said quickly, and drew
his chair to him and sat down. He was busy, and
could hardly afford to spend more time in talking.
The child had got her book; she was provided with
amusement; she might let him alone now and take
her leave.

So he thought, perhaps; but the dark eyes looked
wistfully towards him as he took his seat. They
looked first at him, then at the door, and there was a
few moments' silence, and then, all at once—

. "I suppose I mightn't stay here?" she said almost
supplicatingly.

"Here?" He lifted up his head with a look of
alarm. "Well, I am afraid—" he began, with considerable hesitation.

"I could be quite quiet, you know—if you would
let me sit by the window." A little pause. "Of
course I would go if you like, but—" pathetically—
"it is so much nicer here than in the parlour."

"Then stay here for a little," he said. "I am
afraid it will be dull for you, because I must get on
with my work now, but if you really think you would
like to stay—"

. "Oh yes, I should, very much!"

"Very well then. Find a seat and begin your
book."

Mr. Erle gave this order rather brusquely. A more
civil man would have worded it differently, and would

probably have accommodated Hilda with the chair
she needed; but, to tell the truth, his temper had got
a little ruffled. He could not quite bring himself to
tell the child to go away, and yet he was put out by
her desire to stay. He was accustomed to have his
study to himself; it was a sanctum which even his
mother invaded only rarely; he was not a man who
could work with interruptions or disturbances about
him. He retained a lively recollection of the way in
which Hilda had chattered two days ago when he had
been rash enough in his pity for her to invite her to
look at her pictures in his room. She had made all
work for him that morning impossible. Probably, he
thought, she meditated doing the same thing now,
and he said to himself, with some perhaps not unna-
tural irritation—that he would not have her do it. If
she began to talk he must silence her at once. So,
after his direction to her to begin her book, he bent over
his desk, and took up his pen, resolved that should
she speak another word he would put a stop to her
chattering sharply.

But happily for her, she did not speak another
word. She was a little more used to silence and
obedience than Mr. Erle gave her credit for being, for
she had lived in a school-room too long not to have
learnt how to hold her tongue when she was ordered
to hold it. She sat down beside the window, and
opened her book and read, and remained mute as a

mouse. Her position was almost at Mr. Erle's back, so that without looking round he could scarcely see her; he began to do his work, and after a time he almost forgot her presence. They neither of them moved or spoke again till, when an hour or more had passed, Mrs. Erle once more—just as she had done on the previous day— came with an amazed face into the room.

"Hilda, my dear! I really think—" she began. abruptly.

She had just returned home and was bonneted and shawled. "Where is Miss Ford?" she had asked the servant downstairs, when she had found no trace of Hilda in the parlour; but the servant had known nothing about Miss Ford, except that she had been singing a great deal on the stairs some time ago. "Oh dear, what an anxiety she is to me!" thought Mrs. Erle upon that. "Singing on the stairs while Michael is at work! And now I do believe she has gone to teaze him again in his room!" And so, with quite a cloud of vexation on her brow, the poor soul had come panting up to the study, and had opened the door with these half angry words.

But Hilda looked up with her innocent eyes, and—

"Oh, I am not doing any harm, am I?" she said. "You only told me not to interrupt him, and I have not been interrupting him. I have just been sitting here reading. Haven't I been quiet?" and she turned to Mr. Erle appealingly.

"Yes, perfectly quiet. She is quite right, mother. She has not been interrupting me," Mr. Erle said.

"But, my dear, I would rather that she sat downstairs," said Mrs. Erle rather stiffly.

"It doesn't signify."

"I beg your pardon, Michael. I think it *does* signify."

And then there was rather an awkward pause, which Hilda was the first to break.

The colour had come into Hilda's face at Mrs. Erle's last words, but it was only a flush of anger, not colour from any other feeling. She had liked her morning, and she was angry with Mrs. Erle for finding fault with how she had spent it. She was angry at being found fault with, but angrier a good deal at the prospect of being interfered with for the future in her scheme of establishing herself at will in the study window. The window was so pretty—it was the one pretty place in the house, and she liked to sit in it. Why should Mrs. Erle step in like this and tell her—just to vex her—that she was not to come here any more?

"I do so dislike to sit downstairs! It is so very very dull in the parlour. And I don't think Mr. Erle minds my being here. You don't mind it really—do you?" cried Hilda, with her beseeching face.

He had turned round a little from his desk—
rather unwisely, perhaps—and had now no longer his
back to her, but could see the trembling eager lips,
and the flushed cheek. Possibly, if he had remained
seated as he was before, in spite of her appeal, he
would have sided with his mother, and have told her
that, all things considered, she had better leave him
to the undisturbed possession of his room; but he
saw the poor little face as she spoke, and its pathetic
eloquence was too much for him. In very truth he
would have preferred to have her stay downstairs;
but he was a kindly-natured man, and he could not
bear to tell her so.

"If you like it, I don't object to your sitting here
occasionally. I think she had better do as she likes,
mother," he said, in a deprecating, half uneasy tone.

"Oh, well, of course it is as *you* like," replied Mrs.
Erle, coldly; and then she pursed her lips a little, and
walked out of the room again, leaving one at least of
the two who remained behind a good deal vexed and
ill at ease.

But that one was not Hilda. Hilda, like the
child she was, only plumed herself inwardly on her
victory; and as the door closed, settled herself to read
her book once more with perfect satisfaction and
equanimity.

"But, Michael," said his mother to him later in
the day, "it really won't do; it is absurd; she has no

sort of business to go and sit with you. I really
can't understand how she has no feeling about it herself. I could no more at her age have done what she
has been doing to-day——"

"No; most people at her age wouldn't do it," Mr.
Erle assented quietly.

"It is a sort of thing that offends me; it isn't
womanly."

"But she is not a woman."

"She ought to be a woman, my dear; she is
seventeen, and if at that age she doesn't know that
she has ceased to be a child——"

"Well, of course, most girls of seventeen would
know it; but if she does not, I really don't see that it
matters much. We had better take her as she is.
She is, at any rate, simple now, and free from self-
consciousness."

"And so I am to understand that you mean to go
on encouraging her to spend her mornings sitting in
your study?"

There had come a little silence, and then Mrs.
Erle said this, and, kind-hearted woman though she
was, she said it not a little sharply.

"I have not the least intention of encouraging her,
mother."

"But you mean to permit it?"

"Her being there occasionally will do no harm.
No one could have sat more quietly than she did to-

day. And she likes the room; she likes looking out at the window, poor child!"

"Well, Michael, you must, of course, take your own way. I think you are wrong—and I think Hilda shows a great want of proper delicacy of feeling; but I have got old-fashioned notions, I suppose," said Mrs. Erle, shortly, and took up her knitting and began to click her needles briskly.

"My only feeling is that it is of no consequence. I merely say, if she likes to come upstairs, let her come. Whatever her age may be, she is really a child and not a woman, and so it seems to me that we had better let her do the things that a child might."

And then Mr. Erle, thinking that he had spoken wisely, left the room, and Mrs. Erle, remaining by herself, shook her head over her knitting needles.

"He is very foolish—very foolish," she said to herself. "If it was for nothing more than the look of the thing I should dislike it, but the look is only a small part of the evil. Dear me, I do think that in some things he is as great a child as she is!" And Mrs. Erle gave a sigh, and shook her head again more than once.

———

CHAPTER IV.

MRS. ERLE might shake her head, however, but small good came of that exercise. Perhaps in time, had no counter influence been at work, she might have produced some effect upon her son by doing it, for her son loved her, and was in most things very obedient to her; but upon Hilda she produced, and was capable of producing, no effect by it at all. Hilda, with the selfishness of youth, had in fact few objects in view at this time of her life but one, and that one to follow her own will, and do the things she liked to do, without much regard to other people, and make herself happy as she best could in her own way. Why should she stay downstairs in that dull parlour of Mrs. Erle's, simply because Mrs. Erle wanted her to stay there? She opened her childish eyes round and wide when her godmother tried one day to impress upon her that that lower apartment, and not her son's study, was the proper place for her to sit in.

"But if he does not mind my sitting with him?" she asked, with such an innocent face that Mrs. Erle became confused, and did not know what to say next.

"My dear, *he* may not mind it in the least," she had begun, uneasily, when Hilda interrupted her.

"Then if *he* doesn't mind it, and *I* like it, why do you think that I shouldn't go on doing it?" she exclaimed. "You see I do like it so much. I know you are afraid I shall disturb him at his work," said Hilda, looking as guileless as a dove, "but indeed I don't; I sit just like a mouse. Oh, indeed I don't interrupt him! He always says so, because I ask him every day."

For, by this time, various other days had passed, and Hilda had ensconced herself more than once or twice in the study window. On the day after she had first read her novel there she had gone upstairs to the door and tapped, and when Mr. Erle opened it to her—

"I left my book here yesterday. May I come in and get it?" she said, standing demurely on the threshold.

"Yes, surely. There it is," he said.

And then she silently went forward and took it.

She took it up, and stood still for a moment or two. He had risen, and was standing too.

"How far have you got on with it?" he asked her.

She took the volume to him instantly.

"I was just beginning this chapter, where Lucy

and her father go to see old Alice. I think it is going to be a lovely book!"

"Yes, I have no doubt you will like it."

"Only it will make me very miserable, I suppose?"

"Probably it will."

"I get so very miserable over sad books."

She had transferred the volume to his hands, and seemed, to tell the truth, in no haste to reclaim it. She stood beside him, looking at it vacantly, as if it was no part of her business to take it back; and *he* stood—well, I suppose he had no choice but to stand and hold it till she relieved him.

"I like Ravenswood so very, very much; and Lucy is nice, too. What is it that happens to her? I don't mind being told."

"But I mind telling you. Read the book, and you will see what happens to her."

"But I should like to know. Does she die?"

"Something worse than that."

"Worse than dying?" opening her eyes wide. "Oh dear!"

"Are you afraid to go on with it now?"

"No, I *must* go on. But I can't think what it can be!"

"Well, go on reading, and you will soon find out." And then Mr. Erle, thinking, perhaps, that he had held the volume long enough, offered it back to her.

She took it slowly, with a meekly uttered "Thank

you," and a little sigh—a sigh just so loud as to be
audible to him, and to give him an uneasy feeling as
if he was being unkind to her. Suddenly, too, when
she had sighed, her eyes met his, and in those eyes
there was a look of childish entreaty. "May I not
stay?" they said, as plainly as eyes could speak; and
he stood silent for a moment as he saw them, and
then (what else could he do?)—

"Are you going back to your yesterday's place?"
he abruptly said.

"Over there? Oh, may I?" And all her face
became bright in a moment.

"If you like."

"I should like it better than anything."

And after that in another minute she was safe
where she wanted to be.

Before she went away that morning she prudently
paved the way for her return on the next day.

"If I don't interrupt you, should you mind my
coming again?" she asked him wistfully, standing beside his table before she left the room.

"You sit so quietly, that I could hardly mind it,"
he replied. "I had no idea a few days ago that you
could be so quiet."

"Oh, you didn't know!"

"So I see."

"But now that you do know, may I come back?"
And then the petitioning eyes went up to his face,

and, after only an instant's silence, Mr. Erle answered,
"If you like."

So next day she went back; and on most days
after that one, at some period, though not at the same
period always, between morning and night, her tap
came to the study door. It soon grew to be a very
familiar sound to him; in a degree, too, it even grew
to be a pleasant sound. This grave man of five and
thirty, a student, a hard worker, a man whose life had
in it little that was beautiful, and a good deal that
was depressing, and that took out of him much of
whatever natural light he might once have had—this
man, reserved and grave though he was, could hardly
day after day have his room haunted by a child like
Hilda Ford, and continue to be wholly indifferent to
her. She came to him at first when he did not want
her, but presently he ceased not to want her. He
came almost to like her presence near him. She
always sat in the same place; and often when she was
there she was so quiet, that a soft rustle of her dress,
or a momentary movement of her foot upon the floor,
for an hour together might be the only sign he had
to remind him that she was in the room. His own
seat was always turned away from her, so that her
presence only gave him a sense of something living
near him, except when now and then she broke the
silence by asking some question of him, as she would
do occasionally in an impulsive childish way, or when,

at her coming or going, they talked together for a few moments.

Often these talks were very short indeed—a mere sentence or two on either side if he was busy, and no more; but sometimes they lasted longer. She, like the little chatterbox that she was, would always have been content to lengthen them, yet she was very docile, and submitted to be suppressed and silenced when he chose to silence her. She sat and contentedly read her Waverley novels one after another. With what *he* did while she read she gave herself for a good while little concern. She liked him, but it was her own entertainment and not his work that had any interest for her.

In the midst of a dull environment one must amuse oneself somehow!—how else could the long days pass? Hilda, in open opposition to Mrs. Erle, had carried her point, and made good her footing in the study; yet she had done it in so simple, quiet, childish a way, that who (except Mrs. Erle) could have found fault with her? She had only wanted to get her own way—and she had got it. What was the harm of that? There seemed no harm to *her* in it whatever; it seemed, on the contrary, to her the most natural thing to do in all the world. What else should she do if she wanted a thing than try to get it—as a kitten would—quite regardless of other people? Hilda, with her childish eyes, looked straight into Mrs. Erle's face

at the end of that second morning on which she had
sat reading the Bride of Lammermoor in the study,
and frankly told her what she had been doing.

"Mr. Erle let me stay, and I never spoke a word to
him," she said. "When I don't speak to him it can't
disturb him to have me there—can it? and I like sitting at that pretty window so very much."

Upon which Mrs. Erle cleared her throat, and—

"Yes, the window is very pretty, my dear, very
pretty," she said uneasily. And then somehow, with
the girl's frank young eyes upon her, she could not
go on to express what more she felt. Would not
more harm than good be done by trying to arouse
self-consciousness in a creature who was such a child?
She half thought this as she held her peace. She was
such an absolute child, in spite of her seventeen
years!

And so Hilda in this matter got her own will,
and, perfectly conscious that she had got it, went
lightly on her way, rejoicing. Day after day she came
to the study door and tapped, and always when the
door was opened the bright figure stood for a moment
in the opening, looking like a sweet framed picture,
waiting for her invitation before she entered farther.
It was only a trick she took to—a foolish pretty thing
that she fell into the way of doing. She used to
knock and open the door, and then stand still, not
coming a step forward till he spoke. He always lifted

5*

up his head and looked at her, and said some word
or two; she always on her side looked full at him,
waiting to smile until their eyes had met. It was a
very innocent thing to do—a childish thing, he thought.
A grown woman would have come in differently, if
she had come at all. He came before many days
to think that he liked this simple way of Hilda's
best.

One morning, when she had been sitting with him
for an hour or so, she looked up at him, and said
suddenly, and almost pettishly, "How you move about
to-day!"

"Do I disturb you?" he asked, with a laugh; for
indeed he had been restless enough since she had
come into the room, and had risen from his seat again
and again in search of now one book and now another
from his shelves.

"I can't think why you don't sit still," she said.

"Because I am looking for something that I can't
find."

"Oh!—and haven't you found it yet?"

"Not yet."

"What is it?" she said, after a moment; but the
question was asked rather indifferently.

"A date."

"Only a date!" with marked contempt.

"Do you think that dates are things of no importance?"

"Oh, I suppose some are of importance; but I am sure a great many are not. We used to learn such a number at Miss Fielding's."

"I dare say." But Mr. Erle was turning over the leaves of another book, and answered absently.

She went on reading for a few minutes, then the little head suddenly rose again.

"What do you want dates for? Is it—is it for something you are writing?"

"Yes."

"I wonder what you write?" a little shyly.

"Nothing that you would care to read."

"Shouldn't I? Not any of it?"

"Very little of it, I am afraid."

"Oh! Is it—so very dry?"

"A good deal of it. Not quite the whole, perhaps. I have been writing something this morning, for instance, that perhaps you might like a little."

"Might I?" with some appearance of interest.

"Yes, because it is a story."

"A story!" opening her eyes wide.

"I don't mean a novel, you know," with a laugh. "But I have been telling a story."

"Oh!" a good deal puzzled.

"And it is rather a pretty one."

"Is it?" dubiously.

"You don't seem inclined to believe that."

"Oh yes, I am," colouring a little; "only I should never have supposed that you wrote stories."

"I don't write stories out of my head, but this is a true one. It is all in this book," laying his hand on a volume by his side. "Some day, if you like, you can read it there."

"But if it is all in that book, why are you writing it again?" with a face more full of perplexity than ever.

"Because I am reviewing the book."

"Oh, is that what you do?"

"Review books? Yes."

"I didn't know. I thought you wrote books of your own."

"No."

"Wouldn't you rather do that?"

"Yes, perhaps; but one can't always do the things one likes best."

"I am sure I would write a book if I were you."

"If you were me you would probably do just what I am doing now."

Mr. Erle sat down at his desk again, and took up his pen, and Hilda had learnt by this time that when Mr. Erle took up his pen he meant her to be silent. So she bent over her novel again and left him for the next quarter of an hour in peace. But at the end of that time a little pile of books, which had been standing at his elbow, through some movement that he made, got a sudden push that sent them over on the ground, and as they fell Hilda sprang to her feet.

"Let me pick them up!" she exclaimed. "Don't you move. You have been moving about so much. Just sit still and let me do it. Here they are! Two—four—six—and here is another. That is the whole of them, isn't it?"

"Yes, I think that is the whole. Thank you."

"Where are you going to put them now? You have so many things upon the table. There is no room for them anywhere."

"Yes, there is. They will stand here very well."

"They will just be tumbling down again."

"I will take care of that."

"I can't think why you keep your table in such a litter! Don't you ever clear it?"

"Yes, sometimes."

"I am sure it wants clearing now."

"Don't you take it into your head to clear it."

"I couldn't, because I shouldn't know where to put the things; but I should like to. Is that the story?" abruptly pointing at the manuscript on Mr. Erle's desk.

"Yes."

A little pause; then, suddenly again, and rather doubtfully,

"Might I read it?"

"What I have been writing, do you mean?"

"Yes; you said I should like it."

"You had better read the book itself."

"Oh, but that would take so much time."

"And are you short of time?"

"N—o; but one can't read everything—and that is such a big book."

"Well," with a laugh, "you can read this, if you like. But you needn't burden yourself with it all. I will give you the bit I was speaking of."

He turned over the manuscript, and separating three or four pages from the rest, handed them to her.

"You will find the story there," he said.

"Thank you."

She took the leaves and went back with them to her seat, and began to read them; but after three or four minutes' silence—"There is a break here," she exclaimed, and looked up.

"Yes, that is for an extract. I haven't copied it out yet, but I will give it to you here in the book."

He gave it to her, and she went on reading to the end in silence. When she had finished she sat without speaking for a little while, then she rose up and took both manuscript and book back to him.

"That is a beautiful story," she said.

"Yes."

"Only it was dreadful for the man to have to kill his horse."

"It was the kindest thing he could do."

"Yes; but when the creature was struggling so to get out of the water, oh! I could never have done it."

"He couldn't get out, you see. His master's shot gave him the quickest death."

"Poor horse!"

"And poor master, too. Don't you think so?"

"Oh yes, it was far the worst for him."

And then a little silence; after which, all at once,

"Are you going to copy that piece out of the book?"

"The piece I gave you to read? Yes."

"Couldn't somebody——" hesitating—"couldn't somebody else do it for you?"

"There is no reason why anybody else *should* do it for me."

"But it takes up your time."

"Yes, a little of it."

"I wish you would let *me* copy it."

"You are very kind." Said not very graciously.

"I should like to do it so much; and I can write very clearly."

"Thank you; but there is no need for you to do it. Don't think of troubling yourself."

"Do you think the printers would mind if I did?"

He could not but laugh, the question was so childishly absurd.

"Not unless you wrote so badly that you made your manuscript illegible."

"But I shouldn't do that."

"Wouldn't you let me try?" after a little pause. "Just for once?"

She was standing by his table, leaning both her hands upon it, and looking with those frank eyes of hers full into his face. How could he go on saying No to her, whether he wished to go on saying No or not?

"Of course you may do it, if you would really like. It will be a help to me. I have no doubt that you will do it perfectly well," he said, when he was forced to make his resistance cease. And then the little face brightened all over in a moment.

"I'll go and get my writing-case, then; and I may sit over there, mayn't I? That will be delightful. Will you give me paper?—and I have got my own pen. I will be back in a minute," she said, and away she ran.

In a very few minutes she had got herself established to her liking, and she wrote for half an hour without uttering a word. At the end of that time she presented herself at Mr. Erle's table again, with her manuscript in her hand.

"I have done it," she said.

"Have you done the whole of it? That is very

kind of you." He took the pages and glanced at them. "It looks very well."

"Do you think they will be able to read it?"

"What—the printers? Yes, I think they will hardly find fault with it."

"I tried to make it as distinct as I could. But look—I wrote two wrong words there, and I didn't spell this name right at first. Do you think that will matter?"

"Not in the least."

"And—will you really send it?" looking very eager and rather incredulous.

"Send it? Certainly. What else do you think I should do with it?"

"Along with yours? And they will actually print it?" breaking into a little laugh. "Oh, that is nice! It makes one feel almost—almost as if one was an author! *Isn't* it nice?" she repeated.

"To feel like an author?"

"Yes—and to be doing new kinds of things. I like so to do new things. Will you let me make some more extracts for you?"

"Well, you know, if you go on making extracts, the novelty of doing them will soon come to an end. I think you had better rest content with your first effort at authorship."

"Oh no!" in a tone of disappointment. "You don't mean that really, do you?"

"Making extracts is very dull work.. If I gave you another one to do, I should find you yawning over it."

"No, you wouldn't. I am sure you wouldn't. Don't you believe me?"

"I quite believe you—in one sense."

"But don't you believe me in all senses?"

"No."

"You think I should get tired?"

"I am sure you would get tired."

"Just try me!" drawing herself up, and looking very eager.

"But I have no other extract for you to make— none, at least, just now."

"You will have more to-morrow, though, won't you?"

"Possibly."

"And will you let me do them then?"

"We will wait till to-morrow comes, and then see what mind you are in."

"Why do you say that?" quickly. "Just as if I was a child!"

"Why shouldn't I say it? Do you never change your mind? Do you always want to do to-morrow what you care to do to-day?"

"Yes, I think so." Said in a very dignified way, but yet with a just perceptible want of confidence in the tone.

"Well, I am glad to hear it."

"Why?" rather suspiciously.

"Because it is a good thing to have a steadfast mind." He looked up with a laugh. "Don't you think it is?" And then, without waiting for her to answer, he took up his pen, and "Go away again now to your book," he said; "I must go on writing. Thank you for having made this copy for me." And then he bent over his table, and, finding there was no more entertainment to be got out of him, she did as he bade her, and went away and resumed her reading.

That day Hilda did no further work for Mr. Erle; but she was a persistent little soul, obstinate, wilful, fond of making herself of importance; and if he thought that her first attempt at helping him in his labour would be enough for her, and that she would limit herself for the future in his room to the reading of her novels, he was wholly wrong.

She had begun by this time to have a feeling of decided liking for him. He was not very amusing. Hilda herself was lively, and liked lively people, and Mr. Erle was often silent, and rarely anything but grave; but he was kind to her; he was patient with her interruptions of his work; he treated her in a way that somehow suited her. She did not quite know why she liked either it or him, but she did like both. She was happier when she was with him than when she was with Mrs. Erle. She was not tolerant enough or old enough to have any sympathy with Mrs. Erle. Her godmother's conversation wearied Hilda; she took no interest in it. She thought that Mrs. Erle was dull and tiresome: her commonplacedness and conventionality were distasteful to the girl; her love of propriety irritated her. But Mr. Erle did not irritate her, and when she talked to Mr. Erle she did not get tired and yawn. "I like him because he likes me," she used to say to herself; and it was true that he liked her; but then he only liked her because she had set herself to make him do it. She had almost in so many words appealed to him to be good to her. How, after that, could he have treated her in any way but kindly, or—pretty as she was—have failed to like her in some degree?

"I think, for my own part, Michael, that she has been very strangely brought up in some respects. I never before knew a girl of her age conduct herself so like a child," his mother would say sometimes to him in a more than half-vexed way. But Mr. Erle had always some excuse to make for Hilda.

"I don't know why she should not do what is natural to her; there is no harm in it. Most girls are too precocious: she had far better, I think, be too little of a woman at seventeen than too much of one," he would reply.

And as for Hilda herself, of course she knew that the mother condemned, and that the son upheld her.

Half child as she was, she knew that as well as she knew that the sun shone at noonday.

If she had had anything better to entertain herself with she would have meddled little, as you may imagine, with Michael Erle; but the dulness of her present life drove her to seek for amusement where, had circumstances been different, she never would have sought it. "I can't sit downstairs all day by myself with nobody to speak to—can I? and you know Mrs. Erle doesn't care for at all the same kind of things that I do," she said one day to Mr. Erle pathetically, with an implied assumption that he, on his part, in this last respect, was quite unlike his mother, which he might either take to be complimentary or the reverse, as he chose. Perhaps he did take it to be complimentary. He was in the habit of smiling at Hilda and calling her a child, but at five or six and thirty a grave man possibly would rather be told that he could care for some of the things that a young girl cared for, than be assumed to be too old to have any sympathy left with youth and folly.

He would, indeed, to tell the truth, have been a good deal better content if Hilda had not taken it into her head to begin to concern herself with his work, and to imagine that, with mutual advantage to herself and him, she could contrive to have a hand in it. He was accustomed to do his work in his own

way, and not to be disturbed in it by feminine interference, and the prospect of such interference was
not pleasant to him. After Hilda had copied out her
first extract, he said to himself that he would not
have that kind of thing begun: he could not take any
help from her that would be of real service to him,
and he had no mind during his hours of work to play
at getting help. Probably she would soon tire of so
much as desiring to write for him; but, even if she
did not tire, he would not have the thing done, he
said. So when Hilda came into the study on the
morning after she had done her first piece of writing
for him, and, pausing at his table, after leave had
been given her to enter, asked him with her childish
face if he was going to give her some more copying
to do to-day, he said "No" to her rather shortly.

"No, you may go to your novel with quite an un-
divided mind. I shall not have anything for you," he
said.

And then he looked up, and suddenly saw the
opened eyes and the disappointed, half-tremulous
mouth, and, even before she spoke, felt his resolution
half give way. For, indeed, the worst of it was that
she did not speak. She only looked at him with that
disappointed face, and then turned to go, without a
word. Why did he not let her go as he had intended
that she should, and read her novel, and tease him no
more with proffers of help that he did not want? In

very truth he did not want her help; and yet, when she turned from him in that hurt, silent way, he looked quickly up and stopped her.

"I only wanted one other extract out of that book, and I made it myself last night," he said. "Thank you very much; but, you see, I needn't take up your time."

"It was unkind of you—when you knew I wanted to do it!"

She said this after a moment's silence, in a tre-mulous, reproachful voice.

"I didn't mean to be unkind. I don't think I *was* unkind."

"What harm would it have done you to have let me do it? You knew that I liked doing the other— and it was such a little thing to ask."

She was standing with a flush upon her face, and with something in her eyes so suspiciously like tears that, as Mr. Erle looked up and saw them, the sight gave him a little stab.

"You must not be vexed. I am very sorry. I had no idea that you really cared about it," he said quickly.

"I am sure you might have seen that I cared."

And then she turned away. Without another syllable she went to her usual seat, and Mr. Erle was left to go on with his work.

But he could not go on with his work with any

comfort. He took up his pen, and tried to begin to write; but the thoughts he wanted would not come to him: nothing would come but the thought of the child's reproachful face, and *that* came and would not go away. He had resolved yesterday that he would not have her write for him, and his resolution when he made it had seemed so reasonable a one, and so easy to be carried out; but how could he have known yesterday that, when he denied her what she wanted, her mouth would begin to quiver and those childish tears to come to her eyes? These were things the possibility of which had never occurred to him, but the actual happening of which upset him curiously.

He sat with his pen in his hand, trying to think of the next sentence that he had to write; but do what he would, he could not think of it. He was a kind-hearted man, and the thought that he had grieved the child vexed him. He sat still for five minutes after she had gone away; then all at once he rose up, and, making an excuse of taking down some book from one of his shelves, as he went back with it to the table he stopped at her side and spoke to her.

"Which of your novels is it you are reading now? Count Robert of Paris? I am afraid you will find that rather a dull one."

"Yes—it's dreadfully dull."

She said this in a self-pitying, injured way, without lifting up her eyes.

"Why do you go on with it, then? Let me choose another for you."

"No, I don't want another."

"Why not?"

"I'm going away presently."

"Are you going out?"

"No."

"What are you going to do, then?"

"Nothing."

Mr. Erle stood silent, puzzled what to do next. He wanted to say something kind to her; but how could he say anything kind when she kept her eyes fixed upon her book, and would only answer him in single words? He began to rub his chin perplexedly and to knit his brows. He was not a man who had had much experience in dealing with feminine moods.

"I think it would be a very good thing if you *would* go out a little more," he began again, after a minute's silence. "You don't go out nearly as much as you ought to do, I am afraid."

"How can I go out?" This was asked suddenly, in a petulant way. "I have nowhere to go to."

"Do you mean that we have got no good walks here? I think you are wrong. Have you ever been out yet on that road past the old church?"

"No."

6*

"You would find it very pretty. And then there is another walk round by St. Mary's Hill—and down by the river, too. We are not ill off for walks."

No reply.

"It is very fine this morning. Why should you not go out and explore one of them?"

"By myself?"

She looked suddenly up into his face, with her eyes as round as saucers.

"Can you not go out by yourself?"

"And take long country walks? No, I should think not! I am sure you might know that," in a tone of dignified rebuke.

"Well, if you can't go by yourself, of course that makes a difficulty. I wish you had some companion. I think perhaps my mother might find somebody to go out with you."

"I don't want anybody to go out with me." She said this suddenly and sharply. "I suppose you will propose next to hire a nursemaid for me!"

"But if you can't go out alone, you do want somebody."

There was a little pause, and then all at once—

"Don't *you* ever go out—for walks, I mean?" she asked, with her childish eyes raised suddenly to his face.

"I don't go out for walks often—I have not time; but—yes, I sometimes go."

"You might show me those places."

This was a frank request—so frank that it took Mr. Erle aback. There was a perceptible pause before he asked, rather awkwardly,

"Would you go to them with me?"

"Yes—I suppose so." But she said this with no expression whatever, as if the words had merely dropped from her mouth.

"I can seldom go out till evening. I could not go with you now."

"Evening would do very well."

"We will take some fine evening, then, and have a walk somewhere."

"I dare say it will be fine to-night."

"Should you like to go to-night?"

"Yes."

"I don't know if I can manage it"—hesitating—"but—well, I will try."

"I think you might manage it. I haven't had a real walk all these three weeks," plaintively.

"Well, I *will* manage it. And now what are you going to do? Are you not going to let me get you another book and give up this one?"

"No," rather fretfully.

"Do you mean to go on with Count Robert then?"

"No, I don't want to read at all."

Another pause; then, all at once, with her eyes again upon his face,

"Are you not really going to give me any more copying to do at all?"

They were such reproachful, appealing, wistful eyes. How could he look at them, and tell her that he would not let her do what she wished? He felt ashamed of himself, as he might have done if he had been vexing some child for his own pleasure. The thing she wanted was a thing of so little consequence: she was foolish to care about it, and to continue to harp upon it; but yet, if she *did* care about it, how could he go on refusing to let her have her own way?

"Do you really want to do more copying?" he asked her.

"You know I do"—said almost tremulously.

"But you would find it the dullest work."

"Never mind. I want to do it."

"Well, of course if you wish it, I will let you do it."

"Oh, that is kind!"

"But I really have nothing that I can give you this morning. I can only keep the next extracts for you that I want."

"Oh!" rather disappointed. "And when will that be?"

"Not for a few days, I am afraid."

"And is there nothing I can do till then?"

"No writing, do you mean?"

"Well, writing—or anything."

"I don't know," doubtfully, and rubbing his chin again. "I have a packet of proofs here," after a moment's silence. "Did you ever help anybody to correct proofs?"

"No!" looking very eager and hopeful. "May I try?"

"I am not at all sure that you will like it; but, if you choose, you may try."

"Oh, that will be nice!"—brightening and dimpling all over.

"You will have to sit here by my table; and now, look—you must hold the manuscript, and follow it while I read."

"And tell you when they have printed it wrong? Oh yes, I know!"—in high glee.

"But you must be very careful, remember. You must not let a single mistake pass."

"Very well." But this sobered her a little. "Shall I sit here? You won't read very fast, will you?"

"No, not very fast."

"In case I shouldn't see the mistakes, you know. What would happen"—a little uneasily—"if—if I didn't notice any of them?"

He laughed. "Nothing very serious. You will see that I shall notice most of them myself."

"Oh, I am glad of that! Are you going to begin now?"

"Yes, if you are ready."

And then he began; and with her keen little face on the alert, and her eyes upon the written pages, she followed him as he read.

She was quick enough, and careful enough, too, when she chose: she did not do her part of this first proof-correcting ill. Of course she took more trouble over it than was in any way necessary, and sat with her eyes fastened on the MS., and whenever she was happy enough to detect a blunder announced it with an explosive eagerness that made Mr. Erle laugh, and altogether got flushed and a little nervous over the whole business; but yet the hour that they spent upon it was not at all an unsuccessful one.

"I think it's very nice; it's nicer even than copying, because, you see, it's more exciting," she said when her labours were ended.

"I am afraid I have passed beyond the stage of finding it exciting," he answered with a laugh.

"Oh, have you? Well, I suppose one would in time; but it is exciting to *me*. It's such fun to be looking out for all the wrong things. And, do you know, once or twice I lost my place, and I was in such a fright! I called out to you once, you remember?"

"I think you called out to me a good deal oftener than once. You are a most conscientious follower."

"Am I?" looking very bright.

"Yes—you let nothing pass you. There were several things there, you know, that I shouldn't have noticed if it had not been for you."

"Shouldn't you really? Oh, I am glad of that. Then you will let me do proofs with you again, won't you?"

"If you like—some day when you are inclined."

"Oh, I should always be inclined."

"Don't make rash declarations."

"But I should! I know it quite well. I like to do things with other people."

"Poor child!—do you?"

"Because it is so much more cheerful, you know. Of course, when one is at school one is always doing things with other people, and it seems so odd here to have nobody to do anything with. I hope you will let me go on doing your proofs with you? You will —won't you?"

"If it would be any pleasure to you." He did not want to say this; but yet how could he help saying it?

"Oh, it will be a great pleasure; and then I am to copy extracts, too, you know."

"Yes."

"And we are going to have a walk to-night," with a little laugh. Then, suddenly, "What o'clock is it?"

"A quarter-past twelve."

"Then dinner won't come for an hour, and so I think I *will* give up Count Robert now, and begin another book, if you will choose one for me, please. Choose a very nice one—one as nice as the Bride of Lammermoor."

"I don't know if I can do that—not one, I mean, that *you* will like so well; but suppose you try The Heart of Mid-Lothian."

"Is that a good one?"

"A very good one?"

"Thank you; then I will."

And she took her book, and at last Mr. Erle was permitted to go back to his article.

She was contented enough with the way in which she had spent her morning; whether he was equally satisfied with it was another question, less easily answered, possibly. He had been made to do one or two things that he had not meant by any means to do, and promises had been wrested from him that he had by no means meant to make. It was not probable that the effecting of these things could have pleased him much; yet—little as he might be satisfied with what he had either done or promised—I think as he sat down and began his writing his feeling was not less kindly to Hilda herself. She had teazed him, and

upset his plans, and pressed herself upon him against
his will, in a way that, could Mrs. Erle have been a
witness of it, would have made that good woman's
hair stand on end; but yet, as he once or twice
glanced round at the little figure bending over its
book, the look in his eyes was not the look a man
gives to anything he does not like. He glanced at
her as he might have done at some child whose foolish ways touched him, and whom he was half fond of.
How could a creature of that sort make a man angry?
She was sitting with all her hair about her neck, with
her little flushed face bent down to read the book
upon her knees. She was dark, with a warm gipsy-
colouring—a small, bright little thing. Some people
never saw any beauty in her. Perhaps Mr. Erle had
seen none at first, but now the keen eager face had
begun to have a certain charm for him. "I suppose
that she is hardly pretty; but she is suggestive of
prettiness. She is very picturesque," he had said to
his mother a day or two before. On the afternoon of
this day he told Mrs. Erle that he was going out
with her.

"I am going to show her the walk to St. Mary's
Hill. I suppose you would be afraid to come with
us?" he said.

"Well, my dear, it is further than I ever walk—
but if you and Hilda are going—ahem!——"

"Oh, pray don't come with us if you would rather

not," interrupted Hilda anxiously. "Is it a long walk? I didn't know."

"I am afraid it would be too long for you, mother. You could not walk there and back."

"No, I am afraid I couldn't"—rather stiffly.

And then nothing more was said; and Hilda presently, quite aware that Mrs. Erle disapproved of what she was doing, went upstairs and put her bonnet on.

It was a bright July evening, warm and soft.

"I have never been out once after tea until now since I came here! Oh, I do so like to be out in summer evenings, and to come home after dusk—don't you?" cried Hilda, tripping at Mr. Erle's side as they left the house together. He was a tall man, and she a little woman: she had to take two steps to one of his.

"Yes, it is the pleasantest part of the day undoubtedly. I am afraid we have treated you very badly in giving you no evening walks before now."

"Oh, it doesn't matter." (Hilda was happy, and, enjoying the present, had no time to waste regrets upon the past.) "Are we going this way?—going to turn our backs right upon the town? Oh, I am glad of that! I have never been down here before."

"After a little way the road gets very pretty. You see where the trees rise over there? That is where we are going, if you can walk so far."

"Oh, I can walk anywhere. You don't know what

a good walker I am. I dare say I could tire *you*—because you go out so little, you know."

"I go out a good deal more than you have been doing of late."

"Oh yes!"—with a sudden accent of self-pity—"but then I have never been out so little in all my life as since I came here. This is pretty—isn't it? Look at those lime trees! Oh, Mr. Erle, look how full of flower those lime trees are!"

She walked on by his side, chattering almost without ceasing—asking him questions, calling his attention to everything they passed, breaking every now and then, like a bird, into little snatches of singing. They left the town behind them after a little way, and the road they followed rose gradually higher and higher. It was a pretty, wooded country road. They met few people: they walked in the lengthening shadows of the trees.

"We shall reach the top in time to see the sun set," Mr. Erle said once.

"Shall we? Oh, that will be nice! And then, shall we sit down?" asked Hilda. "I am so fond of sitting on the grass. Aren't you?"

"Yes, I dare say it is very pleasant," replied Mr. Erle courteously, but with perhaps rather a lack of enthusiasm in his tone.

Hilda, however, did not notice it, and when they reached the hill-top she deposited herself immediately upon the turf, and he had no choice but to take his place beside her.

The sun was sinking low, but he had not set yet. From the point that they had reached they looked down over a wide expanse of country, wooded, undulating, peaceful, rich with yellowing corn-fields. "Oh, it is lovely!" Hilda said, and then almost for the first time she fell into silence for a little while. She sat leaning her elbows on her knees, and propping up her chin upon the palm of her hand. That dark little face of hers could lose its childish look sometimes, and another kind of look could come into it, that was womanly and sweet and grave. As she sat without speaking that graver look came now.

He said something to her after a little while about the colours in the clouds, and then presently they began to talk again, and went on talking for a long time. Something that she asked him led to his telling her a story of a thing that had happened to him long ago, and she listened and asked questions, and made other stories follow that first one. The sun set, and they watched the sky grow crimson; and then clear yellow light came in the west, and Mr. Erle rose up and suggested that the grass was growing damp.

"Is it, do you think? Well, I dare say it is; but it has been very nice—hasn't it?" Hilda said.

And then she also got upon her feet. There were

mists down in the hollow; in the town the lights were all appearing.

"I hope we shall come again. I have enjoyed it so very much. Haven't you?" said Hilda, with her frank eyes.

And then he said, Yes, he had enjoyed it too; and so they turned and went down the hill.

It was nearly dark when they got home, and the lamp was burning in the parlour, and Mrs. Erle was knitting by the light of it.

"You must have had a very long walk," she said, and looked up at them over her spectacles as they entered.

"Not so very long; but we sat down on the hill, and waited for the sun to set, and it was beautiful!" Hilda exclaimed.

Mr. Erle sat down with a book, and Hilda, after a minute, went upstairs to take her bonnet off.

"I wonder you kept that child so late out, Michael," his mother said shortly when she had left the room. "There is nothing too foolish for *her* to do, but, really, *you* at your age might be wiser."

"It isn't really late," he merely said.

As for Hilda, she was singing softly to herself as she untied her bonnet-strings and brushed her hair. She had discovered two new entertainments since morning, and the finding of them had made her glad.

CHAPTER V.

"HILDA!" said Mrs. Erle uneasily.

"Yes?" answered Hilda indolently.

"My dear, you have been a month in the house, and, do you know, I have never yet seen a needle in your hand."

"No, I dare say not. I've got nothing to sew," said Hilda.

"But I think you *must* have something to sew. Do you never—do you never mend your stockings?"

"Oh yes—we used to mend them at school."

"But they must wear out all the same now, though you have left school."

"Yes, I suppose they do," with a yawn. "But I can buy new ones. I've got plenty of money, so I may as well buy stockings with it as anything else. Look at all I've got, Mrs. Erle," and she took her purse from her pocket, and began to shake out sovereigns into her lap. "Three, four, five—and I have more upstairs. Oh no, I don't see any good in mending old clothes. I hate mending: I hate sewing altogether," said Hilda.

"My dear, I am very sorry to hear it. I think

every woman ought to try and cultivate a taste for needlework."

But Hilda only shrugged her shoulders. She was sitting curled up in a corner of the parlour sofa, with a pair of scissors in her hand, and her lap filled with paper shavings. She was very fond of cutting out figures in paper, and she did it rather cleverly. She had made a likeness of Mrs. Erle so the other day, at which even Mrs. Erle herself had laughed. Why should she leave this occupation, which she liked, to go to that other one that Mrs. Erle had spoken of?

The girl knew that she was not likely to be ever under the necessity of darning her old clothing. She came of wealthy people: her brother was rich;. she should be rich when she was one-and-twenty. Mrs. Erle, who was poor, might need to trouble herself with small economies; but from Hilda why should any small economies be required? She preferred to cut out her paper figures, to ramble singing about the rooms, to read her novels sitting with Mr. Erle.

I am afraid that, up to this time, Mrs. Erle had not received much satisfaction from Hilda's presence in the house. She and Hilda did not work well together: the girl's idleness, and indifference, and flightiness vexed her. They did not sympathize with one another—they looked on life with too dissimilar eyes.

"She is attractive enough, no doubt, in a certain

way, but I am afraid it is all a surface attractiveness,"
Mrs. Erle would say sometimes to her son. "I begin
to suspect that there is very little that is either good
or high in her. She is very selfish, I am afraid; I
don't know whether she has much heart. Yes, she is
bright and pretty and graceful; that is all very true;
but the fact is, I can't get on with her, my dear.
Other people may be able to understand her better.
It may be all my fault—but I can only say that, if
there is good in her, she lets very little of it come out
to me."

And this was the truth. There *was* good in
Hilda, but somehow she rarely showed it to Mrs.
Erle.

She showed it more to other people. She had
shown it to Miss Fielding, till she had stolen gradually
into one of the warmest corners of Miss Fielding's
heart. She had shown it years ago to her brother; in
a degree, she was showing it now to Michael Erle.
He never went along with his mother when she talked
to him of Hilda. He hardly in words disputed her
judgment of the girl, but he did not agree with it, and
Mrs. Erle knew that he did not agree with it, and I
am afraid that that knowledge did not tend to make
her more charitable to Hilda. It could hardly indeed
have been otherwise. Her son was her one supreme
interest in the world, and she was jealous over him,
and ill at ease when their opinions clashed. They

lived in great harmony when they lived alone with one another, and now Hilda had come into the house, Mrs. Erle felt like a sudden discord which broke and marred their harmony. How could she like her when she did this? or, pretty and graceful though she might be, how could she be in charity with her?

But Hilda, undiscerning or indifferent, still wore her childish face, and went her own way, seeking such entertainment as she could find. Was there any harm in what she did? She only wanted to be amused—to gain something else than weariness from the long days. No doubt she did not consider Mrs. Erle: she placidly did things to please herself though she knew they would not please her godmother; but her moral sense was not much disturbed by that. For why should not she, who had the nature of a kitten, be free, like a kitten, to play in her own way?

She knew very well that Mrs. Erle did not like her to sit upstairs in the study, but nevertheless every morning she slipped upstairs and sat there; and I am afraid, too, that as she grew familiar with the place, and as whatever slight awe she had had in the beginning of Michael Erle wore gradually off, her presence there became less and less of a peaceful presence. She had sat at first mute as a mouse, and he had been able to do his work undisturbed while she did her reading; but after two or three weeks had passed she was by no means disposed to sit wholly mute. She

would still come into the room demure as ever, but
before she had been seated for half an hour the chances
were that she would have made an excuse for speaking to him; and when she had once begun to talk,
unless he chose to silence her peremptorily, he might
as well lay down his pen, for further writing for a
good while to come was rendered impossible. She
would sit with her book upon her knees and with her
face turned to him, letting questions and remarks
follow one another from her lips without cessation,
like water rippling from a spring.

It was a state of matters such as, a few weeks ago,
Mr. Erle would have declared with consternation to
be unendurable, but yet—such strange things do we
learn to submit to—now that it had come, he did *not*
find it unendurable. For several hours daily his soli-
tude was invaded, his peace was disturbed, his work
was interrupted, and yet he bore it all without com-
plaint. He might have complained to Mrs. Erle, and
have insisted on Hilda being kept in the lower regions
of the house: he might have spoken sharply to Hilda
herself, and have forced her to understand that if she
sat in his room she must be silent there; but he did
not do either of these things. To his mother he never
betrayed by a word that the girl disturbed him; to
Hilda, he never gave more than a temporary gentle
admonition to silence. "I am very busy to-day: we
must not talk," he would say to her sometimes; and

then — for she was not wholly without a sense of obedience—she would sit quiet as in the first days, and permit him to do his work. But at other times he let her have her own way. As far as was possible he arranged his occupations so that such portions as needed least attention should be those he did when she was with him. He could read in her presence more easily than he could write, so he fell into the way of reading in the mornings, and reserving a good part of his other work to be done at night, often when she was fast asleep.

Why, in all this, was he so good to her? If you had asked him, perhaps he could not have told you; but he was the sort of man whose nature led him to do things of this sort. A kindly nature, tender and unselfish. He was a man who would have let a pet cat sit upon his shoulder and weigh his arm down when he wanted it to write with, not because he liked to have the creature there, but because *it* liked to come, and he was too kindly to disturb it: a man who would have stopped his work when he was busiest if a child had come to his side and asked him to do something for it—who did slight, unselfish things instinctively.

He had not liked Hilda's coming to his study at the first, but he had submitted to it then because he saw it pleased her. That had been at the beginning, when she had been quiet—a presence in the room, but not necessarily a disturbing presence. Afterwards, when she lost her shyness, and broke in with so little compunction on his peace, he might well have lost patience with her, and have let her know that his occupations would not bear such interruption; but he did not lose patience. She chattered to him as no feminine lips had ever chattered in that room before, and he merely laid his book down and listened to her.

Of course, when he did this he had begun to like the little rippling voice; he had begun to find it pleasant to look up and see the bright young face. When he sat writing at his desk he could not see her; but often when he read he turned his chair half round, and his eyes would rest on her at times when she was quiet, gently and almost tenderly. He was five-and-thirty, and graver and older than men often are at that age; she was seventeen, and almost a child. Sometimes in these early days, when he stood beside her, he almost felt as if he might have put his hand upon her head, as though she had been a child in very truth.

After that first morning when she had helped him to correct his proofs, she never without her assistance let him correct any proofs again. He had to submit to do them all in conjunction with her.

"You won't do them alone? You promise me you won't?" she said.

She asked him this a day or two after they had

done their first piece of work together, and he had to laugh and promise that he would not. "Unless you are out of reach, or get tired of helping me. I *must* do them without you then," he said.

"Oh, I shall not get tired, and I am almost never out of reach, you know; or when I am, you can wait for me. You will wait, won't you? And you will give me all your extracts to do?"

"No, not all, because I want to do some of them myself."

"Oh, you don't?" And then she put on a pleading face. "You don't want to do any of them?"

"You shall do all the little ones, if you like, and I will do all the long ones."

"No, no!"

"You won't do the little ones?"

"I won't do the little ones, and leave the others for you. You don't mean that?" looking quite distressed and reproachful.

"How are you to get on with your novels if you copy out all my long extracts?"

"I have plenty of time for both. I have so much time, that I don't know what to do with it."

"You might turn it to far better account, then, than by writing for me."

"I am sure I couldn't!"

"You might read something better than novels.

You might go on with some of the work you were doing at school. Why don't you?"

"Because I have done with being at school now" —half deprecatingly, as feeling that the answer was a very foolish one, but a little defiantly, too.

"And with education altogether, do you mean?"

And then she began to look childlike and supplicating.

"Oh, please don't talk about education! Of course I am not educated—I know that; and it seems very dreadful to you, I dare say. But what is the good of it? What is the good to *me*, I mean? I don't care about learning: it will never make me any better than I am. Who would ever care for me the least bit more in the world if I knew history, or geography, or arithmetic, or any of those things that I don't know now? Perhaps—perhaps *you* would," said Hilda, with her frank, childish eyes, "but I am sure ninety-nine people in a hundred wouldn't."

He made no answer to this speech, and there was a little silence, and then —

"That was what I always used to tell Miss Fielding," she said.

"That there was no use in your learning anything? And what used she to answer?"

"Oh, of course she couldn't let me see that she agreed with me, because she was a schoolmistress; but I know that in her heart she did."

"And you think, perhaps, that in my heart *I* do?"

"I don't know," a little dubiously. But she looked at him speculatively as she spoke, and after a moment they both laughed.

"So, if I can't do anything better, I may copy out your extracts for you, mayn't I?" she said.

It is not only those who are strong who get their own way in the world: the weak as well as the strong gain it, the foolish as well as the wise; perhaps, even, on the whole, the strong and the wise gain it, or at least take it, seldomer than the rest. These foolish Hildas—*they* get their own will when the people who are better than they stand aside and let them push past.

This poor little Hilda Ford did not push forward on her path roughly; but do you think, when she saw a thing she wanted to reach before her, that she did not try with all her soul to reach it? She saw it, and desired it, and made her way to it, working towards it sometimes as a worm works through an old book.

It was so dull in this quiet house; what could she do in it but try to amuse herself with Michael Erle? What harm could come of doing that? He had known her when she was a little child—before she could more than barely remember him.

"I can just recollect your coming once when we lived at Riverside," she had told him, "and you took me on your shoulder and carried me round the garden.

Do you remember? I must have been less than six then, for when I was six we left that house; and how old were you?"

"If you were six, I must have been twenty-four."

"Oh dear, what a great age! And you have been living on here ever since?" And then she looked at him as she might have looked at one of the patriarchs.

As if to show, too, how much of a child she was, she had made him call her by her name. She always spoke to him as "Mr. Erle;" but one day, when he addressed her as "Miss Ford," she pettishly asked him what he meant by it.

"I am sure, when you carried me round the garden, you didn't call me 'Miss Ford,'" she said.

"Probably not," he answered.

"Then why should you do it now, when you have known me all my life?"

And then after that he had to call her "Hilda." At least he called her so when he called her anything at all; but he did not speak to her often by her name.

She used to do so many childish things. She asked him one day to tie a ribbon for her that bound her hair. She used to appeal to him about her dress, and make him notice it, and tell her the colours that he liked; and when she knew these colours, she would wear them. Why should she not wear them when he thought them pretty, and she liked to look well in his eyes?

Then she made him take walks with her. After that first evening on which he had taken her to St. Mary's Hill he often went out with her: he hardly had it in his power to do otherwise, for she used to ask him to go. "Mrs. Erle is not strong enough to take walks, and I can't go by myself. You will go with me, won't you?" she would say to him coaxingly; and then, what could he do but go? Whenever he had leisure enough to make it possible for him to spare the time he went with her: he often, indeed, went with her, because she asked him, when he could very ill spare the time.

"You are getting into the habit of sitting up later and later, Michael," his mother began to say to him. "The day used to be long enough for you to work in, but now you seem to want the night too." And when Mrs. Erle said this I do not know that he had ever any satisfactory answer to make to her, for it was quite true that he was falling into the way of sitting up for hours after the other members of the household were asleep. How could he help it?—for how could he have the heart to tell the child, when she appealed to him to talk to her, or walk with her, or amuse her, that he was busy and could not do what she wished?

Once or twice he told her so, and then he could

not bear her look of disappointment. One evening
he had promised to go somewhere with her, and just
as they were about to start a messenger came unex-
pectedly with some work for him to do, and he told
her that he could not go.

"I am very sorry, but I am afraid you must take
your walk alone," he said to her. "It will be as
much as I can manage to get this done by to-morrow
morning."

And then he looked at her, and saw that the tears
had sprung to her dark eyes.

"Oh, you might come!—just for a little way. I
won't go by myself. What is the good of going by
myself?" she began to exclaim plaintively. "I was
counting so on going. Just come for a little, little
bit—because it has been so dull all day, you know."

It had not on that special day been a bit more
dull than on twenty days before, but she said that it
had, and he was credulous enough half to believe
her.

"Well, if we are to go at all, let us start at once,"
he said. "We must really only go a little way; but I
don't like you not to have your walk."

And then she brightened up, the sunshine coming
back, and the clouds dispersing again in a moment,
in that April way of hers: and she had her walk, and
he sat up afterwards and worked till the day began
to dawn.

Occasionally, in these summer evenings, they used to have grave and quiet talks together. She did not quite at all times chatter nothing but nonsense to him. Sometimes she would be content to put away her childishness, and let his humour lead her; or even of herself she would at moments fall into a mood that had some wisdom and womanliness in it. She had a true enough sense of beauty, and often when they were out together the loveliness of the quiet summer country seemed to touch her. She liked to turn her back upon the town, and get out of the streets into the fields; she had a simple natural love for flowers and trees.

"I think I should be good if I lived always in a pretty place," she said to him once. "That is why I like to come up to your room so much, because it is so pretty there, and one seems free from all the mean, small, vexing things. I don't like little, vexing things. I wonder why women's lives generally are so full of them!"

She was never grave for long together, but the suddenness with which at times she changed from gay to grave gave these occasional moods a charm that, perhaps, they might have scarcely had if they had come more often. For we tire a little of constant sameness, even when the quality of it is excellent; there is piquancy in light and shade—and Hilda at least was piquante, whatever else she failed to be.

CHAPTER VI.

SHE had to give up her seat in the window when the colder weather began. "I sha'n't get any other seat half so nice," she said plaintively on the first day when a fire was lighted; but nevertheless she submitted to deposit herself in a cosy corner by the fireside, and presently took to that new place kindly enough. It was warm, and she liked warmth—it was comfortable, and she was fond of comfort: she was a luxurious little soul, this child Hilda.

"I can't think how people do who can't get fires," she would say sometimes, in these cold days, bending down to warm her hands till the blaze made a flush on the little face. "I am so glad I am not poor! If I were to be poor it would kill me, I think."

"I am very glad you are not poor; but still I don't think it would kill you if you were," Mr. Erle told her once.

"Oh, you don't know. You don't know how miserable I should be."

"But people don't die because they are miserable."

"I think I should."

"Why should you more than any one else?"
And then of course she could not tell him.

"Oh, I should feel it so. Some people feel things so much more than others. I always feel things dreadfully," was all she could say.

And, in a sense, that was true, for she did feel all things that touched herself very keenly. She was very quick to suffer, very sensitive. She was quite right when she said that she should be miserable if she were poor, for hers was a sensuous nature; and the thought of poverty, and of the mean troubles, the sordid pains, that poverty entails, was hateful to her. She would have taken more root in this new home of hers if it had been a richer home; she would have cared more for Mrs. Erle if Mrs. Erle had had no need to count the shillings in her purse. She hated to count shillings; she hated economy and thrift. It was partly because in Mr. Erle's room she had less sense than elsewhere of the household's straitened means that she liked to sit in that room best. It was true that he worked there, and had to work hard; but at least he did not pore over account books, as his mother did, and docket bills. These were the mean things of the doing of which Hilda was intolerant—things that she had no sympathy with, that seemed to make life miserable.

Mr. Erle used to let her talk a great deal of folly to him; but yet at times, too, he would rebuke her, and she took his rebukes on the whole not impatiently. She was pretty well accustomed, indeed, to be found fault with, in a tender way—to be laughed at and corrected, and told that she was foolish. Miss Fielding, who loved her, had done this for years, and so rebuke had come to seem a familiar thing to Hilda. She was quite used to it, and I am afraid, too, that she was a little hardened to it. Advice, correction, schooling of all kinds, she took as innocuous medicine, that satisfied the giver, and to herself did little or no harm. "Try to guide her as you will, she will pass through life going her own way," Miss Fielding used to say of her, very truly.

Probably, too, as time went on, Mr. Erle also found out this. He did not know much about women, but he came to understand that this slight, bright creature had come, not either to be taught by him or to teach him, not either to be made better or worse by him, but simply to sing beside him like a soulless bird. If he had opened the window and some lark had flown in from the outer air and burst into its clear light song above his head, it would have been much the same sort of thing. Could he teach her or influence her any more than he could touch that bird with its wild, sweet voice? She used to seem as though she came so near to him; and yet how strange a distance there often was between them! Could she enter into the thoughts that were in his heart? Could she see life, or the world around her, as he saw them? Sometimes, for a moment or two, it used to seem as if some light of sudden comprehension came into her, and the dark eyes would grow deep and passionate, and she would say some word or two that might have come out of another heart than hers—as if an angel had passed by her, and in passing had touched her lips. But a second would change all that, and bring her back again to her common mood—to her bird's song and her kittenish play.

"I am sure, Michael, she must often worry you," Mrs. Erle would say sometimes to her son.

Mrs. Erle had given up contending with her, and long before the cold weather came Hilda had got it all her own way in that matter of sitting in the study; but yet, though she had ceased to interfere, none the less was Mrs. Erle's mind disturbed, and her temper tried by Hilda's wilfulness. Again and again she would preach to the girl about the importance to her son of peace and silence while he worked, and Hilda, looking meek as a dove, would answer "yes" to everything she said, and then half an hour afterwards would be seated in the study, Mrs. Erle's sermon and her own assent to it both forgotten, chattering like a magpie. If Mr. Erle let her talk, what did it matter to any one else? that was what she thought. She liked to talk; and she had not perched herself in that

room of his for many weeks before she knew well
enough that he liked her to talk too.

For in truth it came to that: he got to like her
foolish chatter; he got to like the sight of the childish
face, and the sound of her voice, and the echo of her
step upon his floor. She disturbed his work, but he
bore that; she talked to him often when he was
busiest, and he endured that, too; she was not an un-
obtrusive presence in his room; she made herself felt;
she filled the room with a sense of life—and he submitted to it all.

"I wonder if you ever wish that I wouldn't come?
Do you?" she said to him one day.

"What would be the use of my wishing it? You
would go on coming, I suppose, all the same," he answered with a laugh; and perhaps he philosophically
endeavoured to reconcile himself to her presence
through this belief; but yet I scarcely imagine that *she*
thought he did.

"Yes, you prevent my work; you disturb me very
much; you are a great hindrance to me," he would
tell her sometimes; but when he did that he was always speaking in jest—he only half meant her to believe him; and she would receive his assertions with
a perfectly unembarrassed laugh.

"It must be very dull never to be disturbed. I
am sure you were very dull before I came—were you
not?" she said to him once; and when he did not an-

swer instantly—"Now, were you not? And won't you be dull again when I go away?" she quickly asked.

"No, I don't think I was dull," he replied boldly then. "I got my work much more quickly done. I was able to go to bed at a reasonable hour in those days, and get a good night's sleep."

"I dare say you slept too much," she retorted saucily.

"Well, possibly I did. At any rate, you have altered that. I don't sleep too much now."

And then she laughed.

"*I* get eight hours' sleep always. I couldn't do with less. You, poor thing, I don't think *you* almost get five," she said.

But she minded very little, though she shortened his time of rest. Small misdeeds sit lightly on the consciences of creatures like Hilda Ford. She did not mind though she disturbed him and took up his time: the only thing she minded was lest Mrs. Erle should find out that she did these things. Mrs. Erle made domiciliary visits to the study sometimes; and if on any of these occasions Hilda was found to be chattering (a thing that would happen!), the girl would bite her lips with vexation.

"I know Mrs. Erle thinks I am always talking; and I am *not* always talking—am I?" she said, on one of these days, eagerly and appealingly to Mr. Erle. "I

am sure I had not opened my lips for an hour till
just before she came in. If she says anything to you,
you will tell her that. Won't you tell her? or else she
will scold me, and try to keep me away."

"Yes, I will tell her if you like; but I am sure she
doesn't often scold you," Mr. Erle replied.

"Well, perhaps she doesn't scold me, but she talks
to me, you know, and that is just as bad; and I don't
deserve to be talked to to-day—do I?—when I had
been sitting so very still."

But little *contretemps* of this sort cannot be
avoided always, and on the whole I think, if Hilda
was undeservedly rebuked once or twice by Mrs. Erle,
she escaped rebuke so many times when she had
fairly earned it, that her sense of injustice in the
treatment awarded her need hardly have been very
keen.

"No, my mother will not keep you away. I like you
to be here," Mr. Erle said to her once.

It was a slight thing to say, yet it meant more
coming from him than it would have done from the
lips of many others, for he was a reserved man, who
did not often put what he felt into words. Quiet, too,
as the sentence was, it was the first direct approval of
her presence that he had ever given her; and when he
spoke it, she made no answer to him—you might almost have thought, perhaps, that she did not notice it;
but she did notice it, and she remembered it. She loved

approval too well not to do that. She loved to make herself of importance — to be cared for where she went. Possibly she had known well enough before this day that Mr. Erle liked her, but the spoken words were welcome to her for all that. The vain little heart took hold of them, and held them, and cared for them.

In the winter days that came on after this time they fell gradually into a habit of having long and often grave talks together, or, rather, he for the first time began to talk in those days to her. Hitherto it had been she mainly who had chattered, and he who had listened, sometimes saying little, sometimes answering her, but doing nothing more; but now—almost as if the sombre season of the year had brought the change and made it appear natural—he fell, perhaps unconsciously, into taking a part in their conversations that he had not done before; and often after this it was he who principally talked, and she who listened, or seemed to listen, to him. They used to sit together over the fire, and he would tell things to her—things that he was reading, or things that he had done or thought. He was a silent man usually; and she with her bird-like nature had little in her, one might have thought, to have tempted such a man out of his natural mood, and yet, somehow, he ceased to be silent when he was with her. Unlike as they were, there was, perhaps, some sympathy between them—

something that made her content to listen, even when she did not understand him—that made him content to talk, even when he knew that half of what he said passed lightly and uncomprehended over her. They liked one another, and that liking, I suppose, was the common link between them. They were so dissimilar, that after a time their very dissimilarity, perhaps, attracted them to each other. He was a sensible man, but he came to like her almost for her folly's sake; she was so foolish, and yet there was so often something in her that was as the germ out of which a soul might spring.

It was this, indeed, I think, that in a large measure gave her charm to her—this vague, uncertain, indefinable promise of something that might be yet to come; a promise as of pure sky behind obscuring clouds which till now had only rifts in them, but that some day (you thought) might disperse and leave the heavens clear. It was a delusive promise; but, perhaps, as he gradually came to care for her more, there were at least moments when he almost trusted in it, and believed that she might become nobler, better, and higher than she ever did or could.

Of course she took the best seat in his room during these winter days, and established herself without compunction in his armchair by the fire. He, when he drew towards the fire, had to sit in an armless, straight-backed chair, in no superabundant comfort—

but she pitied him for his want of ease once, and then she hardly thought of him any more.

"We ought to have two armchairs, ought we not?" she said. "If I take up this one always I am afraid you will want to get rid of me. Don't you think you will?"

"No, I shall not want to get rid of you—on that account," he replied.

"Not if I keep you out of your place?"

"You are welcome to my place. You look very comfortable in it."

And then she laughed. She *was* comfortable: she was seated at ease; she had her feet upon the fender; she was leaning her head against the chair's tall back. The little figure and the gipsy face looked very pretty in that dark, big framing.

"I like easy-chairs so much. I can't think why people ever make chairs uncomfortable. I can't think why people ever make anything uncomfortable," she said in her pleasure-loving way.

Long before this time it had come to be an uncontested thing that he was to permit her to do certain little services for him—to read his proofs with him, to copy out his extracts, to unpack his new books and cut them open. His work consisted chiefly of reviewing, and new books came to the house often. They were seldom books in which Hilda took any interest, but she always made it her business to undo the

parcels, and be the first to look at their contents.
She took a childish pleasure in doing this, and in
ranging the fresh volumes on his writing-table. She
used to hover round him, quite indifferent to what he
might be about, chattering, and doing her little frag-
ment of work. "Be quiet for a few minutes: I can't
attend to you just now," he might possibly say to her
now and then; but for once that he said this he let
the little chirping voice sound in his ears twenty
times. He was too kindly, perhaps, to interrupt it;
or perhaps he had got to like it too well.

Sometimes she would take an interest in the things
he wrote, and when they read his proofs together
would show a liking for what she read, and ask intel-
ligent questions about it; but she did not take an interest in what he wrote always.

"I wish you didn't review so many dull books,"
she would say to him. "I think that far the greater
number of books are dull, except novels. I can't
think *why* you don't review novels. Shouldn't you
like to?"

"I am afraid not," he said.

"But why not? They are so much nicer than
other books. I am sure if you once began you would
like it—because you are not so very old, you know."
And she looked at him speculatively.

"I am afraid I am too old to begin to take to
novel reading."

"Well, it is a pity," and she gave a sigh. "It seems to me a dreadful pity not to like stories." And for the moment she was genuinely sorry for him. But feelings of most kinds with Hilda did not last long. In another minute she was talking about something else. She had flitted off to a new subject, as a bird flits to a fresh bough.

Ever childish, changeful, fitful, full of humours; and yet, if she had had more sameness in her, would Michael Erle, do you think, or many another man, have liked her better? Without the lights and shadows in her she would have been another Hilda—not this foolish one, but possibly one far better: yet who that ever cared for her would have liked the lights and shadows gone? You took her as she was, or rejected her as she was. There were some people for whom she had no charm; but there were others who, with all her folly, loved her more dearly than if she had been the wisest woman upon earth.

CHAPTER VII.

"I wish you had not to work so hard, Michael," Mrs. Erle said one night.

She gave a sigh as she spoke. She and her son were sitting in the parlour alone together, and he was reading; but when his mother addressed him he put down his book, and looked up.

"I am not working very hard," he said.

"But you were never strong, you know, and you often look so worn now. I think you do your writing more slowly than you used to do, my dear—or else that child disturbs you. I do believe she disturbs you, Michael, though you won't allow it. She talks to you and wastes your time. She is so thoughtless and inconsiderate—and so selfish. I don't want to be hard upon her, but she *is* selfish. She doesn't really care for anything in the world except herself. As for her liking for you, she merely likes you because you let her have her own way."

He said quietly, after a moment or two's silence,

"I don't know how one can help letting her have her own way."

"My dear Michael, that is a very foolish speech to make."

"She is very dull here. There is so little that we can do for her."

"Well, she has got some new friends now."

"Yes."

"And she is likely enough to find them to her mind, for they seem to me very gay and foolish people."

There was a little silence: then Mr. Erle said abruptly,

"Why are you so hard upon her, mother?"

"My dear, I don't want to be hard upon her; but, you see, she vexes me."

"I don't know why she should vex you. You can't make all people alike. You don't quarrel with a flower, because it is a flower and nothing else."

"No, but I quarrel with a woman who thinks she has nothing else to do in life but to make herself like a flower."

And then there was a pause again, and Mr. Erle rose up.

"I am sure, Michael, I wanted to like her before she came here. I was as ready as anybody could be to like her and think well of her," Mrs. Erle said.

"Yes, I know that. I am sure you were."

"It isn't my fault that we have not got on better together."

"I have never thought that it was."

"You mustn't take part with her against me, Michael."

He went to his mother's chair without speaking, and stooped down and kissed her: then he stood for a few minutes beside her with her hand in his.

"I have been almost afraid sometimes of late that you were going to let her come between us."

"You need never fear that."

"Don't do. it, my dear"—with a half sob. "I couldn't bear it."

"You will never have to bear it."

"I have almost wished sometimes that she had never come into the house."

"You should not wish that; she has done no harm."

"But she may do harm yet. She has to be here for six more months. I wish the six months were past."

And then Mr. Erle made no answer, but after a moment or two went away to his own room.

These new acquaintances of Hilda's that they had spoken of were friends of her brother—a Captain Ponsonby and his wife, who had come one day at the beginning of the winter to see Hilda, and had asked her to go presently and stay with them for a week or two; and she had gone now. They had a house ten or twelve miles from where the Erles lived. Captain

Ponsonby had come this morning to fetch her, and she had gone away with him in high delight. For days beforehand she had been talking about her coming visit in a very natural, girlish, happy way. The Ponsonbys were rich, and she was likely to spend a gay time with them, and she was looking forward to parties and dances and all sorts of pleasant things. She had chattered about her new acquaintances to Mr. Erle, until Mr. Erle, who did not know them, might naturally be supposed to have become rather tired of the subject. But if he did he never told her so, and, happily engrossed by her own thoughts and hopes, she never suspected a possible weariness on his side.

"The wife is a very pretty and very fashionable-looking woman, and he is too fine a gentleman a great deal for my taste, but I dare say they will both suit Hilda," Mrs. Erle had said to her son a month ago, giving her account of these new friends after their first call.

"She went away as happy as a queen," she reported to-day. "I don't know what she is looking forward to. I think her head is half turned already, and how she is to settle down here again when she comes back, I am sure I don't know. I shouldn't be sorry, for my own part, if the Ponsonbys were to take a liking to her, and want to keep her; but I am afraid there is little chance of that."

She had run up to the study before she went away to say good-bye to Mr. Erle. Last night she had said to him,

"I wonder if you will ever miss me when I am away! Do you think you will?"

She had asked him this standing beside his table, and poising herself upon it in a childish way that was common to her, looking in his face, too, as she spoke.

"Yes, I think I shall miss you," he had answered.

"You will be so quiet—won't you?—when I am gone. I wonder if you will like it?"

"I don't know. I shall be able to tell you that when you come back."

"I don't want you to like it."

"Don't you?"

"No; because if you were to go away and leave *me* here alone, I shouldn't like it at all."

"Well, happily there is no danger of my doing that."

"No—that is a good thing."

And then the next moment she had begun to speculate about some one of the many things concerning her visit with which her mind was filled, and she thought, or at any rate she said, nothing more about him or his missing of her.

To-day, equipped for her journey, she came into his room as bright as a sunbeam.

"I am going!" she said, standing on the threshold, with the door held wide open in her hand.

She was dressed in some warm, rich colour; the little gipsy face was flushed with excitement. He looked up at her.

"You are going, are you? Well, be very happy. Make all you can of your holiday," he said.

"Oh, of course I shall be happy. But I shall think of you very often."

"I am not so sure of that."

"Oh, I shall! I am quite sure of it. But I mustn't stop. Good-bye." And then she put her hand in his.

"Is Captain Ponsonby waiting for you?—Good-bye," he merely answered. And away she went.

She was as happy as a bird as she skipped down the stairs, and gave her light parting kiss to Mrs. Erle, and jumped into the carriage that was at the door. Was she not going to be borne away into another kind of world than this quiet, dull, and sordid one that she had inhabited for six months—a world that should be full of delights and bright and pleasant things?

"I hope you will forgive me for saying it, but, do you know, I hardly feel as if I envied you your resi-dence with that worthy lady," Captain Ponsonby said to her as the horses started, and the carriage rolled out of the dingy street: and then Hilda laughed.

ι   "No, nobody would envy me, I am afraid. Oh, it
is so dull," she said. "She is very good—she is as
good as she can be; but if you only knew how tired
of her one sometimes gets!"

"I can imagine it. There are few things duller
than goodness," replied Captain Ponsonby.

And then for the next ten minutes he joked about
Mrs. Erle, and Hilda listened and laughed. Was there
any harm in laughing? Her companion was very
amusing, and Hilda did not profess to care for Mrs.
Erle; yet, in spite of her laughter, possibly the girl felt
a little twinge of conscience while Captain Ponsonby
turned her into ridicule.

They drove the whole of the little journey, for the
country was pretty and worth seeing.

"It is rather too long a drive for me to take, but
if you think you would like it, and if you won't mind
having only Captain Ponsonby for your escort, he will
be very happy to come for you on Thursday morning,
and drive you out," Mrs. Ponsonby had said to Hilda
in her note a few days before; and so this arrangement had been made. It was winter, but the weather
was mild, and the sun shone on them pleasantly
enough. Hilda was happy—or she thought that she
was happy—and the time passed quickly to her. Her
companion was kind, and talked to her, and amused
her. Once or twice, as the carriage rolled along, she
wondered what Mr. Erle was doing, but she did not

think of him much; she was too excited to think:
her thoughts stretched forward — they did not turn
back to concern themselves with what she had left
behind. "It has been a delightful drive. I have enjoyed it so much," she told Mrs. Ponsonby when they
reached their journey's end.

The house that she had come to was large and
handsome — a country house standing in its own
grounds. "Yes, it is a pretty enough place," Mrs.
Ponsonby said carelessly to Hilda; "but we are never
here for more than a month or two in the year. In
fact, it is impossible ever to be long anywhere. Everybody's time is so broken up. One must be in London
in the season; then we have visits to pay; then perhaps we come here for a little while; then we go
abroad. I can never stand more than a small part of
an English winter: it kills me. We shall be going to
Italy next month. You have never been in Italy yet,
I suppose? What — never out of England at all? Oh,
I do pity you, then. I think England is a detestable
country. Yes, I am not patriotic at all. I hate dulness, and fogs, and vulgarity. We are such a dreadfully dull, respectable, vulgar people. I have not the
least sympathy with the English character."

"What — not with any of it?" said Hilda, opening
her eyes.

"No; I think the creature we call a John Bull ought
to be swept off the face of the earth. There is no

such vulgarity in the world as English vulgarity—no
such coarseness anywhere else. I ought to know if
any one does, for I have travelled so much, and I am
so sensitive to the sort of thing. No," and Mrs. Ponsonby folded her delicate hands upon her lap, and
looked contemplatively into the fire, "with the excep-
tion of the men and women in the upper ranks, the
English are simply an insupportable nation. As you
grow older, my dear, and have more experience, you
will agree with me. No one with any real refinement
or mind could think otherwise."

She was a very pretty woman, though her first
youth was past—tall, blonde, and aristocratic-looking.
She was talking with Hilda in her boudoir, leaning
back amongst the cushions of her sofa; and Hilda,
from a less luxurious seat, was looking at her and ad-
miring her amazingly. How very handsome she was!
the girl was thinking; how beautifully she was dressed!
what a wonderful fine-lady air she had! Hilda, who,
with all her faults, was not a fine lady at all, looked
with a feeling of awe on the other's grandeur. She
glanced at her own plain dress, and felt ashamed
that it was not finer. Her little heart began to beat
with a feeling of mingled uneasiness, vexation, disappointment. In the dull house whence she had come
her clothes had always looked almost too pretty and
dainty to be in harmony with her surroundings; but
here, all at once, they seemed to have become taste-

less, dowdy, commonplace. Compared with Mrs. Ponsonby's perfect toilette, did her poor dressing even deserve the name of dressing at all? She looked at her merino frock with its plain trimming; she thought of the other frocks in her yet unpacked trunk, and I am afraid the first drop of bitter came into her pleasant cup.

In an indolent, languid way her hostess for a little longer went on talking to her. Mrs. Ponsonby nearly always talked languidly, and, let her words be what they might, uttered them always in a gentle tone—a sign of high breeding that both roused Hilda's admiration and inwardly disturbed her, for Hilda herself was impetuous and impulsive, and rarely said things gently when she felt them much, but blurted them out in a rapid, eager way, quite incompatible with high breeding. The girl almost unconsciously got chilled a little as she sat and listened. Everything about her was so pretty, so delicate, so refined, and yet she felt as if it were all outside her—all too far from her for her to have any part in it; too much above that poor dull working world in which she had been living of late, and which must have dulled and blinded her somehow, she thought, and made her unfit to enjoy this higher and more admirable sphere.

It ought to have been very delightful, she felt, to listen to Mrs. Ponsonby, and yet somehow it was not wholly delightful. Mrs. Ponsonby paid Hilda the

9*

compliment of talking to her indeed, but she talked,
paying no more regard to her personality than if she
had been the sofa on which she sat, and want of
regard for her personality was not a thing that Hilda
had had to submit to much of late. So the girl
somehow got rather depressed as she sat listening.
There was a little envy in her—a little hurt vanity—
an undefined sense of disappointment—a feeling of
anger against herself, for she had expected to be
wholly at home in this new lofty world, and she knew
now that she was not at home in it at all.

She was a little subdued when she betook herself
presently to her own room, and began to think of all
that lay before her. There were other visitors besides
herself in the house. There was a Lady Barker and
her two daughters, and a Mr. Suffern, and a young
man—a Mr. Falkland—who was going out to India
as an engineer.

"Mr. Suffern is a most eligible *parti*, my dear,"
Mrs. Ponsonby had said to her; "only I must warn
you that you mustn't set your cap at him, unless you
want to make an enemy of Lady Barker. Mothers
with marriageable daughters are rather dangerous
persons to be meddled with, you know."

"I am sure *I* shall not meddle with her," replied
Hilda hotly.

"And you mustn't fall in love with Mr. Falkland,
though he is a very charming young man, because,

unfortunately, he is *not* an eligible *parti* at all. He is a great friend of mine, and a most delightful person; but, mind, I shall allow no flirting!"

"I am sure I don't want to flirt," retorted Hilda.

And then she had gone to her own room with her spirits not quite so elated as she had expected that they would be.

However, she was elastic, and she brightened up again presently. She had to dress for dinner, and dressing for dinner was an operation important enough to engross all her thoughts. She was little more than a schoolgirl, you know: she never yet in her life had sat as a guest at a formal dinner party: she was a little afraid of the ordeal that lay before her, and yet she was pleasantly excited by the thought of it, too.

"I suppose they will all be dressed ever so much better than I shall be," she thought to herself with a sigh; "but I can't help it. I think this is a pretty dress, really" (it was a white dress, and was very pretty indeed), "but I suppose it will look dowdy and— common as soon as any of the others come near me. I wish I had something nicer to put on, but I haven't, so there is no good in thinking of it." And then she stood before the swing-glass, and looked at herself, and—"I wonder if anybody will think that I am pretty at all!" she thought. "I dare say not—for I suppose every one else will look better than me; but I wish somebody might." And she looked at herself this way and that, and began to pirouette and curtsey before the long glass till she fell to laughing at last —a fair enough sign that she was not ill pleased at the figure which she saw reflected.

And, in fact, it was a very pretty little figure, plain though the white frock was. Captain Ponsonby thought so for one, when she came into the drawing-room; and fat Mr. Suffern, who was seated at her entrance on a sofa, being ministered to there by one of Lady Barker's daughters, seemed also to be of Captain Ponsonby's opinion, for he opened his half-closed eyes, and followed Hilda with them, as she crossed the room in Mrs. Ponsonby's wake, and then snapped the thread of Miss Barker's discourse by a sudden question.

"Who is that pretty little thing?" he said.

"That girl with Mrs. Ponsonby? Do you call her pretty? She's odd-looking, I think."

"She is pretty in her way. Effective, you know. That's as good as being pretty."

"Oh, do you think so?" And then Miss Barker looked distressed.

"Far better, often."

"Dear me! I don't see that. I think real beauty is better than anything."

"Yes, when you can find it. But where are you to find it? I don't see a beautiful face once in six months."

"Oh, Mr. Suffern!"

"No, nor once in a year sometimes."

"Oh, I never heard of such a thing! Mamma, just listen to what Mr. Suffern is saying."

"What is Mr. Suffern saying, my dear?" asked Lady Barker, and bent forward blandly.

"He says we are all so ugly that we are not worth looking at, and that he doesn't see a pretty woman once in a twelvemonth."

"I think, my dear, Mr. Suffern is jesting."

But nevertheless Lady Barker drew herself up a little; and Mr. Suffern laughed a fat soft laugh.

Hilda was given in charge to a young lieutenant with a stiff white tie to be led in to dinner, and it happened when they took their seats that Mr. Suffern was her neighbour on her other hand.

"Charming weather, isn't it? Have you been walking to-day?" said the lieutenant, who was not staying in the house, but was only dining there.

"No; I have been driving," replied Hilda. "I have driven all the way from Porchester."

"From Porchester, have you? Why, that's my birthplace," said Mr. Suffern on her other hand.

"Oh," responded Hilda, not at all interested.

"Porchester your birthplace. Is it really?" exclaimed Miss Barker. "Dear me! I never imagined that."

"Yes. Curious fact, isn't it? But a man, you

know, *must* be born somewhere. It used to be a smoky old place?" and Mr. Suffern turned again to Hilda.

"It is smoky enough now," said Hilda.

"Not improved in that respect, you think? Well, I dare say not. Do you live there?"

"I am staying there just now."

"In what part?"

"In—in Bell Street."

But Hilda said, "In Bell Street," a little unwillingly, for she was rather ashamed of having to confess at so fine a dinner-table that she was staying in such an unfashionable place.

"Bell Street? I don't remember Bell Street," said Mr. Suffern.

"Oh, I dare say not," said Hilda. "It's a very dull street. The whole town is very dull, I think."

"Let me see—Bell Street?" repeated Mr. Suffern, throwing his eyes up to the ceiling. He was not taking any soup, or else he might have relieved Hilda by giving the point up. "Bell Street! Does it turn out of Royal Terrace?"

"Oh no, it isn't there at all," said Hilda.

"The only Bell Street I can remember is a dingy little street down by the Hospital."

"That is it," said Hilda, colouring.

"That? Oh—ah—I beg your pardon. Oh, to be

sure!" But Mr. Suffern opened his eyes wide for a moment.

"I am only staying there for a little while. I am expecting my brother home from India. I shall live with him when he comes," Hilda said in an uneasy, half explanatory, half deprecating way. For she was ashamed of the discovery that Mr. Suffern had made, and yet she was ashamed of herself for feeling any shame about it; and she felt almost grateful to the young lieutenant when, a few moments afterwards, having taken his soup, he betook himself to the duty of entertaining her again.

On the whole, it was rather a dull hour, perhaps: I am not sure that Hilda enjoyed it much. The lieutenant probably did his best, but his conversational powers were not of a high order, nor was he even gifted with any superabundant liveliness. Poor little Hilda would have liked to talk and be merry if she could, but one cannot talk and be merry without support; and as far as support in such matters went, the lieutenant was a broken reed to rest upon. On her other side was Mr. Suffern, and, after a little period of silence had enabled him to recover from the surprise that her announcement of the place of her abode had caused him, Mr. Suffern began to talk to her again; but tastes are variable and capricious things, and I am not sure that Hilda quite appreciated the blessing thus bestowed upon her.

"Naughty child! naughty child! Did I not tell you not to set your cap at Mr. Suffern?" said Mrs. Ponsonby in a whisper, playfully shaking her fan at her, when they had returned to the drawing-room; and then at this rebuke Hilda flushed up.

"How can you say that I set my cap at him? I don't like him at all; but he *would* talk to me," she cried indignantly. And then the fan reached her lips, and tapped them into silence.

"You foolish little thing—are you going to lose your temper? Why, there is Miss Barker looking like a thunder-cloud, and *you* are going off as if you were a sky-rocket. How am I to keep the peace between you?" And Mrs. Ponsonby shook her head, and went away laughing.

Hilda had only been for a few hours in the house, but these few hours had already given her more than one new experience. Were they pleasant experiences altogether? "I wonder what Mr. Erle is doing!" she thought suddenly to herself, as she sat at the close of the evening over her bedroom fire. "It is only eleven o'clock; I dare say he hasn't finished working yet. I wish I could go and see. I think he is better—ten times over—than all the people here." And then for a moment she almost thought—not quite, but almost —"I wish I was with Mr. Erle again;" and she laid her head down upon her pillow presently, thinking of him. Somehow it seemed better, and it seemed to

make *her* better, to think of him than to think of her
new friends.

The evening had not been a pleasant one to her.
The young ladies of the party had ignored her existence, and Mr. Suffern had pinned her in a corner, and
talked to her in a fat, lazy way, till she had yawned.
And then at half-past ten everybody had taken their
bed-room candles, and the night had come to an end.
But it had been dull; and Hilda, in her heart of
hearts, knew that she would have been happier if, instead of being where she was, she had been sitting in
the study at home with Mr. Erle. For Mr. Erle liked
her, and she liked him, and these people—! "I think
they are such strange kind of people," she had said
already to herself. "The women are so proud and
disagreeable, and the men—oh, I don't like the men!
I don't think I even like Captain Ponsonby very much,
and I wish the others were out of the house. I feel
as if I should only like to touch that Mr. Suffern with
a pair of tongs." And then it was after that that she
suddenly thought to herself, "I wonder what Mr. Erle
is doing! I think he is better than all the people
here."

She thought that he was better than they were this
first night. Afterwards, as time went on, perhaps she
got more accustomed to her new surroundings. To tell
the truth, she *wanted* to like this novel world that she
had come into; she liked its wealth and luxury without

an effort, and she wanted to like all the rest of it—to
like its people if she could, and their thoughts and
ways. And she strove hard to do it too, and thought
sometimes that she had succeeded. One night they
had a dance, and on that occasion she was genuinely
as happy as her heart could wish. Sometimes she
went out riding, and she loved to ride, and always
came in from such expeditions with a bright face.
Occasionally she had a passage at arms with Julia or
Emily Barker; and as she usually came off the victor
from these encounters, they tended, if not to her edi-
fication, at any rate very decidedly to the raising of
her spirits.

But still, in spite of these enjoyments, somehow
Hilda missed the perfect happiness that she had expected to find. It did not make her happy to be
talked to by Mr. Suffern. Mr. Suffern talked to her a
good deal; and, though she did not like him, she let
him do it, because she knew it made Julia Barker
angry; and sometimes she was ashamed of herself because she liked to make Julia Barker angry, but she
went on doing it in spite of being ashamed. "I know
I could never be good here, so it is no use trying,"
she would say to herself. "Nobody is good, or cares
about being good, so I needn't attempt to be better
than the rest of them." And then, though she had
said the first night that she could only bear to touch
Mr. Suffern with a pair of tongs, she would let him

walk with her, and ride with her, and would feel her
spirits rise when she saw poor Julia Barker's clouded
face. "If she had treated me differently I wouldn't
tease her," she said to herself as a sort of excuse for
what she was doing. "If she gets miserable, it is all
her own fault. Why is she such a goose?" And then
Hilda would sharpen the edge of her tongue, and
make her eyes bright, to attract the fat prize that she
did not want, and draw it away from the woman who
did want it dearly.

It was a poor enough game to play, and Hilda in
her heart knew that; but the atmosphere around her
was an atmosphere that encouraged such games, and
so she played it. It amused her too; and had she or
any creature round her at present another object than
to be amused?

And yet even entertainment is sometimes so hard
to find, devote ourselves to the search after it as we
may! If you had asked Hilda, after she had been for
ten days with the Ponsonbys, if she was enjoying her
visit, she would have answered that she was enjoying
it very much indeed, and would have thought that she
was only speaking the truth; and yet she was not,
in fact, more than very partially enjoying it. She had
perhaps, beforehand, anticipated too much pleasure
from it to have her anticipations quite realized. Had
she thought that the people she should associate with
would be better, kinder, more delightful than they

had proved? Had she thought that amongst them she should be of more importance than she found herself to be? She was not of very much importance as it was to any one. Mr. Suffern liked her well enough to follow her about in an indolent way, and the Barkers disliked her enough to say ill-natured things to her; but nobody else in the house paid very much regard to her at all. She was pretty and piquante; but the Barker girls were both handsomer than she was, and the guests who came about the house for the most part admired them more than they did her. They were a pair of fashionable, high-bred young ladies, and she was only a little schoolgirl, very deficient, indeed, in high breeding, and even deficient, unhappily, in the lesser points of ribbons and laces and furbelows. These were lesser points, but they went for a good deal in the new world into which Hilda had come. "I could almost make myself look as pretty as they, if I were dressed like them," the girl would say sometimes to herself with a sigh; but she was not dressed like them, and so they outshone her. And then she took the only revenge it was in her power to take, and flirted with Mr. Suffern.

But, in truth, it did not make her happy to flirt with Mr. Suffern. It was often a very dull amusement; it was at times an amusement that gave her a feeling of disgust and shame; for the man was personally repugnant to her: he was so indolent and fat

and oily. He was not an unkindly-natured man, but
the flesh was predominant in him with an offensive
and unwholesome predominance. He had a double
chin that wagged when he laughed, and dimples in
his soft hands where other men's knuckles show, and
his legs were short, and his figure was loose and
flabby. Hilda used to put the tips of her fingers upon
his when he shook hands with her, and would shirk
doing even that when she could. She would back her
chair when he sat down near to her, and if his coat
sleeve touched her, or, more than that, if by chance,
when perhaps he was showing her some book or picture, his breath for an instant came across her, she
would start away from him as if she had come close
to something unclean. But yet she had nothing else
to do, and so she made Julia Barker jealous by letting
him hang about her. There was a malicious amusement in doing that, and Hilda, under evil influences,
was very capable of being malicious. She had so
many bad or imperfect things in her, this poor foolish
Hilda; it was only the wisest and best influence that
could ever have made her good, or have raised her
above the common level of common-minded women.

But, as I said, she was not more than very partially
happy as these days passed on. She was so far from
being perfectly happy, that one morning, when the
contents of the post-bag were emptied out, and a
letter was handed to her in Mr. Erle's handwriting,

the colour came to her face with the keenest feeling
of pleasure that she had known since she had entered
the Ponsonbys' house; and when she opened the envelope and saw that two lines from Mr. Erle were all
that accompanied the letter from her brother which it
enclosed, the sense of disappointment succeeding to
her gladness was so sharp that she almost could have
cried.

"This letter has just come. I hope you are well
and enjoying your visit. My mother is out, or she
would write," was the whole of Mr. Erle's note.

"He might have written a little bit more, I think.
It isn't kind of him! He might have written and told
me what they were doing," the girl thought in a hurt
way to herself. And then she took up her brother's
letter and opened it, and that, too, had something in
it to vex her, for he wrote—

"It was very kind of the Ponsonbys to call upon
you, but I want you to know that I am not at all
anxious that you should become intimate with them.
If you have not paid your visit by the time this
reaches you, defer it, if you can—and I think you will
be able to do so easily—till I come home. They
belong to a set that I should very little like you to
get yourself mixed up with."

"I don't know what he means by getting 'mixed
up' with them! I am sure staying for a week or two
at a house can matter very little one way or the

other," cried Hilda petulantly to herself when she had read these sentences. And then she gathered up her letters and went away with them, with a sort of hot, unreasonable, injured feeling. She had been so glad when she had seen Mrs. Erle's writing outside the envelope, and then almost in a moment all her gladness had turned into vexation and disappointment. "He might have written something more, and not have sent such a wretched little scrap as that," she said again, when she was alone in her own room, and then she took out the couple of lines, and re-read them, and stood looking at them angrily.

To tell the truth, she thought more about them and their brevity than she did about what her brother had said as to her becoming intimate with the Ponsonbys. If her brother's letter had come when she was on the eve of her visit, she would have been very indignant indeed about it, and probably would have done her very utmost in the face of it to get her visit paid; but now, in her heart, she did not really care much about the Ponsonbys, and her brother's letter moved her less by a good deal than those two lines did of Michael Erle's. Why had he not written something more to her, if he had written at all? She would not have sent two lines like that to him, she thought.

Hilda was only a child yet, you know, and thought,

perhaps, that people always wore their hearts upon their sleeves. Whenever she had been dull or vexed during these last ten days, or whenever she had felt that she was of no importance to these new people round her, she had always half consciously plumed herself and comforted herself in the belief that she was a good deal to Mr. Erle—that he, at least, must have missed her, and would be glad when she went back again: but now he had written these two cold lines to her, and he did not say one word about missing her, nor ask her when she was coming back, nor tell her that it would make him glad to see her. "I care for him ten times more than he does for me. I don't think he cares for me really one bit," said the child to herself, with a quiver at the corner of her lips.

She was not happy during the remainder of that day. She talked a good deal to Mr. Suffern, and said sharp things to him which made his eyes twinkle with lazy admiration under their fat lids: but she was not happy, and still less was she good. "I don't see the use of trying to be good when nobody cares for me," she said to herself bitterly. "I don't think anybody in the world cares for me much, except Miss Fielding. I wish Miss Fielding would come back and ask me to stay with her. At least, I think I do. I'm not sure. I don't know what I wish. I think one gets tired of everything sometimes."

Once, after she had been making some little speech like this to herself, she fell into silence for a long time. She was standing at one of the drawing-room windows, looking out. It was winter, but the sun was shining, the sky was blue; there were flowers still blooming in the garden; there was a sweet wide view stretching across an open country. What a contrast it all was to the narrow street she had to go back to soon! What a contrast these luxurious rooms were to Mrs. Erle's dingy parlour, and her son's study with its littered books! And yet, as the girl stood there, in her inmost heart she knew that she wanted to see that narrow street again—that she could forgive the parlour its dinginess if it would receive her and give a welcome to her—that if she were once more seated in that littered study, in her old place, with Mr. Erle talking to her in his old way, she should be happier than she had been since the day she turned her back upon it all.

"He cared for me, and nobody cares for me here," she said to herself, with that childish self-pity that always came to her so readily. "He did care for me when I came away, whether he forgets it now or not." And then the tears came to her eyes. Like a child she had been confident till now of Mr. Erle's regard, and now, like a child too, all her confidence was shaken at the first fear that she had lost it. "I didn't think he would forget me. I care for him more than

he cares for me. I think it's hard," she kept saying
to herself.

It was after this day that she first began to wish
her visit had come to an end. She had been dull at
times in the course of it before to-day, but yet she
never till now had consciously wished that it was all
over, and that she was at home again. After to-day
she began to do this. The novelty of the thing had
ceased for her, and the days had begun to seem long,
and her thoughts kept wandering curiously back to
·what she had left behind her. If any one had cared
for her here, or made much of her, she would not
have been dull, I dare say: under such circumstances
she would have been pleased and flattered, and the
vain little childish heart would have been content
enough with its surroundings; but, in truth, nobody
cared for her here—not even Mr. Suffern, though he
liked in his lazy way to be amused by her; nobody
cared for her; she was of no importance to any one:
she might stay where she was and nobody would
be glad; she might go away and no one would be
sorry.

And this was a state of things that Hilda did not
like. She was slow to acknowledge that she did not
like it, but after that little note of Mr. Erle's she fairly
confessed it to herself. She was tired, and wanted to
go away. The big house, and the luxury, and all the

signs of wealth around her, were pleasant to her, but yet she wanted to go back again where somebody cared to see her and hear her voice. They were so cold to her here, and all at once this coldness, which she had scarcely felt at first, began to make her dull and weary.

The Ponsonbys had asked her to come to them for two or three weeks, and ten days of this time had passed when Mr. Erle wrote her that little note. She stayed for another week after it came, and then she went home. She had thought at first, innocently, that she must stay for the whole length of her invitation, and perhaps for a little longer: but in the course of her visit she found that no one was at all likely to raise any objection to her taking her departure when she pleased, so one day she said to Mrs. Ponsonby, "I think I ought to write to Mrs. Erle about the day for my going back;" and Mrs. Ponsonby replied at once, "Well, my dear, what day would suit you?" And then Ililda proposed one in the middle of the third week, and the matter was settled at once. Perhaps her vanity was a little hurt that it was settled so easily, but yet, if it was so, something else in her that was better than her vanity made her glad. "Only three days more, and then I shall be at home again!" she began to say to herself. She had never before until now called the Erles' house "home," but during the last week she had begun to do it almost unconsciously. "Only three days more! I wonder if he will like to have me back!" she thought.

She became curiously eager to know whether or not he would be glad during these last days. "Perhaps he won't mind," she said to herself sometimes; but yet, though she said that, and though she was still sore about the coldness of his note to her, still in her heart she did not think that he would not mind. He would not seem specially glad to see her, perhaps, at first—that was not his way—but when she came back to her old place, in the bottom of her heart she thought that he would like it. She thought he would; she hoped he would; she almost felt once or twice that she could not bear it if he did not.

"I am very pleased to have made your acquaintance, my dear, and I hope that after you come out we shall often meet in town," Mrs. Ponsonby said to her with a very sweet smile before they parted. And then she put her white hands on Hilda's shoulders, and kissed her on both cheeks. "It has been very nice to have you here. I have quite enjoyed it," she said languidly.

But the other ladies of the party did not make any profession of this sort when Hilda bade them farewell. Lady Barker and her daughters gave her the tips of their fingers, and said good-bye to her in an altogether simple way. Mr. Suffern had already taken his departure, and one or two other guests had come who neither liked nor disliked Hilda, but merely looked upon her as an unimportant unit in the company. She was not pretty, you see, in any way that would attract much general notice, and she was shy as yet, and not at home in fashionable society. She was so very little in the estimation of all these fine people; and she knew that, and shrank into herself in their presence a good deal more than she liked or wished to do.

So, with a feeling that was made up half of joy and half of vexation and disappointment, she took her seat once more by Captain Ponsonby's side, and he drove her home. Captain Ponsonby was a good-natured man, and he had a kindly enough feeling towards the little girl. He had been kind to her during her visit in a careless off-hand way, and as he drove her home now he chattered to her about fifty different things. "You must come and stop with us again, you know. We must get you over in the summer next time. We will have you and your brother and his wife all together, and we'll get up lots of picnics, and have a jolly time of it," he told her before they parted.

He drove her to the Erles' door, and then bade her good-bye there, and did not come in. "I won't disturb Mrs. Erle," he said, with a twinkle in his eye, and so shook hands with her on the threshold, and mounted into his seat again, and drove away.

And then she was at home again. Her heart was beating fast as the familiar door was opened. It was dusk, but in the gloom as she entered she saw a figure that she knew: another moment, and a friendly hand had met hers.

"You are welcome back again," Mr. Erle said to her.

That was her first greeting. A moment afterwards Mrs. Erle came forward too, and spoke to her, and kissed her. "I am so glad to be back," the girl said quickly. Her face was flushed when they brought her into the lighted parlour. "Oh, I am so glad to be back!" she said again.

"But you have been happy, my dear? You have enjoyed yourself, haven't you?" Mrs. Erle asked; and then she answered—Yes, she had been very happy; it had been very nice, but yet——

How small the room seemed to be! The fire was burning dully; the gas had been turned up too high, and hissed and flared against the glass; there was a kettle singing vulgarly upon the hob. It was all so small and ugly and shabby and poor; and yet, for the first time, Hilda did not mind its narrowness or its poverty. She stood in the strong gaslight, unconscious that it was flaring above her head. She only felt that she had come back again to the place in which she wanted to be; that she was contented to have turned her back upon all the grandeur in which

she had lived of late; contented, and more than contented—happy with a shy happiness that made her
heart beat fast--to be standing once more by Michael
Erle's side.

CHAPTER VIII.

HAD she only been away for such a little while?
"It seems as if it had rather been months than weeks,"
she said to Mr. Erle; and then she thought to herself
(but she did not say aloud), "I am glad it has been
only weeks." For until a short time ago she had still
been counting the months half wearily, and thinking,
"It will be so long yet before Henry comes;" but
now, suddenly and unreasonably, she had begun to
look forward to the time of her brother's coming with
an undefined sense of shrinking and distaste. She
had got used to being here—she liked being here—
she did not want to go away, she had begun to
think.

She fell to thinking this, soon after her return from
the Ponsonbys', in a strange, eager, restless way. She
had come back to her old seat beside the study fire;
she had come back apparently to live her old life in
the Erles' house again; and yet in reality she had *not*
come back to that old life at all, but to a new life
that was wholly different from the old. Outwardly,
indeed—to most people's eyes—there was little enough
change as the months went on, either in it or in her.

To Mrs. Erle she seemed as much of a child as ever
as she went her wilful way, talking foolishly, doing the
things that pleased her, regarding Mrs. Erle and Mrs.
Erle's wishes very lightly. "I don't think she will ever
grow any wiser," Mrs. Erle used to say of her, sagely
shaking her head. "What I feel most strongly, Michael,
is that there is so little material in her to work upon.
I don't know how it is, but she always makes me
think of soap bubbles." And, indeed, there was often
an airy, soulless lightness about her that only too well
justified Mrs. Erle's opinion. But yet this soullessness
was not the whole of her. She had no depth of nature in her, probably; she had no steadfastness; she
had little strength; but, for good or for evil, she had
feeling and passion, at least, if she had nothing else.

"May I come in?" she asked Mr. Erle, standing at
the study door on the morning after she came back
from the Ponsonbys', the dark little gipsy face flushing
up as she put her question; and when he answered
"Yes" and she went in and took her old seat again,
in that moment the old life ended for her, for she
went knowing for the first time that she cared to be
with him more than she cared for any other thing.
Her three weeks' absence from him had taught her
that—a truth which it would have been well that she
had never learnt; for her own sake and for his.

For these two, you see, could never be anything
to one another. They had got thrown together in

these intimate relations who ought never to have been
thrown together. She was rich and he was poor; she
was young and he was almost old; she was here in
his house at all only because her brother had put confidence in him. However dear she might become to
him, he had no right to speak one word of affection
to her; he dared do nothing to make her love him.
He could only be kind to her, as he might have been
kind to any woman whom he liked, and who liked
him. And he *had* been kind to her merely in that
way for six months; but after she came back from the
Ponsonbys' the hard thing for them both was that she
could not endure to have only such kindness from
him any more.

He gave it to her again—for what else could he
give her?—and after a little while she resented it and
refused it passionately, with mute looks and quivering
lips demanding something different from him in the
place of it. Why should he not give her that other
thing which would have made her happy? she began
to say to herself. For, with her childish nature, there
never was a time, either now or later in her life, when,
if she had had it in her power, she would not have
sacrificed the future to the present, recklessly satisfied
to be glad to-day whatever other thing than gladness
might come to her to-morrow. She would have done
this; she could not help doing it. She was born with
only that power of living in the passing moment—as

butterflies live in the sunshine—as the moth lives its
passionate hour of life in the light that ends by
killing it.

She had come back from the Ponsonbys', yearning
for some reaction from the coldness and indifference
that had been round her there, yearning to be loved
and warmed and comforted, and thinking (in as far as
she thought at all) that she had but to return like a
bird to the nest she had left, and let the hand she
trusted give this love and comfort to her. And so
she had returned, shy, eager, full of hope, and had
found——

She had been happy for a few days at first, because it had seemed to her so good a thing to be
beside him once more, that for a little while his old
kindness almost satisfied her; but presently that con-
tentment lessened, and then by degrees it altogether
ceased. She fell again into her old way of spending
half her time beside him, because he let her do it,
and she could not bear to be away from where he
was; but the hours that she so spent often brought
little gladness to her, because she wanted something
that he would not give her, and like a child she could
not rest because it was withheld.

Gradually, when they were together, as the weeks
went on, he grew more and more grave and silent,
and she became sad and quiet too. She rarely showed
any of her old gaiety to him now; they often were for

hours in the same room almost without speaking to
one another. How could he talk to her in the old
way, when he was conscious of the new thing that
had come into her . heart? Very often they were
silent, and sometimes she used to get petulant and
impatient with him. "I suppose you don't want me
to stay here?" "You don't believe I can do anything
to help you?" "Yes, I am only a torment to you; I
don't know why I come near you at all," were sentences that she fell into the way of flinging at him;
and sometimes when she spoke to him in this way he
would not answer her (for it was often so hard to
him to answer her), and one day when he did not
answer her she burst into tears.

That was a day when she had been more than
usually restless and craving for some sign of affection
from him. She had been hovering about his table,
trying to do first one and then another little thing for
him, and he had told her that he did not want them
done, and then all at once she had said something
angrily to him, and when he did not answer that she
burst into those foolish tears. "You never let me do
anything now: you hate to have me here—and I—I—
I can't bear it!" she sobbed.

There she stood before him—the quivering little
figure, with its loose hair and wet flushed cheeks. He
gave one look at her, and turned away. Could she
even conceive how hard it was to him to do that,

when he knew that he had but to have held out his hand to her, and she would have been comforted? But he turned away and said nothing for a moment or two, and then he merely spoke in his ordinary voice.

"You must not let yourself cry just because I tell you not to move my books," he said. "You know that I let you do a great many things for me. I will give you something to do now, if you like, that will really be of use. Look, here are all these letters that want tying up."

He opened a drawer, but she only glanced at it disconsolately.

"I don't want to do them," she said in a weary way.

"Why don't you want to do them?"

"Because you just give them to me to keep me quiet."

"I give them to you because you seem to want something to do."

But she sat down suddenly, and laid her head sadly on his table, without answering him.

And then there was a pause. What could he say more to her? He looked at her; but two, three minutes passed before he broke the silence.

"Are you not well to-day?" he said at last.

"I don't know," she answered listlessly, without changing her position.

"You should not sit like that, as if you were in trouble, when you have nothing to be troubled about."

"How do you know what I have to be troubled about? You don't either know or care," she said bitterly.

"I care very much."

"You don't know what caring for anything means!"

And then there was silence again, and after a few moments he began to read, or seem to read, a book that lay open on his desk.

A little while passed while she remained motion-less, her cheek lying on the hard surface of his table, as if it had been a pillow, and her eyes after a time raised so as to reach his face. She wanted him to speak again to her, but he did not speak, and at last she broke the silence.

"Are you not going to do anything for me?"

This was said in a tone of reproach that was al-most tragic—so nearly tragic that he laughed as he turned round to her.

"What do you want me to do?"

"You might be sorry for me when you see that I am so miserable. You might be sorry," she said hotly, lifting up her head at last, "instead of sitting there and jeering at me."

"You know I am not jeering at you."

"I wouldn't sit and laugh at *you* if you were un-happy."

"You are tired because you have been doing no-thing all the morning. Get a book and read. I will give you something to read."

"No, you needn't; I won't read it."

"What do you want to do, then?"

"I don't know," dejectedly; and then, after a moment, she laid her head down upon the table again.

He returned to his book, and seemed to go on reading, but he did not read it. It was hard to hear her appealing to him, and to have to let her appeal in vain. How could he sit there and not think of what might be if the cruelty of circumstances did not bind him? He seemed to read, but in reality he only saw the little figure with its sunken head, and the weary face that he might not comfort.

There was a long silence, for he was afraid to speak to her again. He never spoke until at last, in her self pity, the tears began to trickle down her cheeks, and she put up her handkerchief to wipe them away. Then he could not be silent any longer.

"You must not do this; you must not sit there and cry," he suddenly said to her. "You think that I am unkind to you. I am not unkind. I would give more than you know to make you happy."

"You wouldn't!" she answered indignantly, with a

passionate sob. "You don't care whether I am happy or not."

"You don't think that."

"I do think it!"

"Come here and let us do something together."

"I don't want to do anything with you."

"What do you want, then?"

She rose up all at once, and gave a look into his face—a piteous look that said something which her lips could not—and then, without a word, turned away. How could he ask her what she wanted? the poor little quivering heart was crying to itself; how could he ask her when he knew she could not tell? For, in truth, she thought that she never told him what she wanted, not knowing that in everything but words she told it to him every day, again and again.

She went away and took refuge in her armchair by the fire, and sat there for a long time doing nothing. He might have followed her, she thought, and have talked to her and comforted her; but he did not follow her. They sat apart, until at last her loneliness got intolerable to her; and then, like a child, she went back to him.

She was penitent then: not angry with him any longer, but only miserable.

"You said we might do something together. Please don't mind my being cross. I am so tired to-day,"

she said plaintively. And then, as he looked up, "I
am so *very* tired. Oh, do talk to me. Don't leave
me by myself; I can't bear it," she said. "Look, just
let me stay here—I like to kneel here—and talk a little
bit to me. Can't you tell me something and make
me good?"

She had a childish way at times of kneeling at
his side. He had tried to prevent her doing it, but
he could not prevent her. She would come and slip
down on her knees beside his chair, and then, leaning
her elbow on his table, would prop her head upon her
hand, and turn her face up to him. Sometimes, when
she could get him to talk to her, she would stay so
for a long time.

She knelt beside him now, and he could not make
her alter her position. "I haven't been disturbing
you so very much? You can spare a little while to
talk to me, can't you?" she said, looking at him with
her wistful eyes: and then, how could he say "No" to
her, or refuse to do the thing she asked?

Women like Hilda Ford are curiously selfish; they
are selfish even where they love most dearly: they are
too like children to be anything else. All through
these months it was of herself that Hilda thought the
most; it was her own love, her own sorrow, that filled
her heart. She cared for Mr. Erle, but she did not
care for him as another kind of woman might, valuing
his happiness so much beyond her own that to secure

it she would give up her own content. To Hilda it was not possible to love any one in that way. She wanted to be happy with him, but she never longed to bring some good thing to him at the cost of a great sacrifice to herself. She was self-absorbed, as children are—loving him, indeed, but always, in spite of her love for him, loving herself and her own happiness best.

He was a man to whom some better woman than Hilda might have given a deeper and worthier affection, if he and any such better woman had been ever thrown together; but it was his fate only to find *her*. A hard enough fate, perhaps, though she never knew it. For she never knew with how light a love she loved him, nor how all impressions and all emotions were temporary with her: swift to come—sharp while they lasted — and swift to pass away. In different circumstances, would she even have ever cared for Michael Erle at all? She thought she would; she thought during these months that wherever they had met she would have loved him; but, in truth, if her life had been less dull, and her days less idle, that foolish, hot, impressionable, faithless heart of hers would never have been quickened in one beat it gave by him.

He, perhaps, knew her better then she knew herself, and read her bright light nature as she herself could not read it. He never loved her for any goodness that he found in her, nor for any constancy that he ever hoped to find. What she was he, perhaps, knew; and what the value was of her love for him,— that, I think, he understood too, and rated it at its true worth—at the worth of the sunshine of a summer day, or of the passing song of some sweet bird.

———

CHAPTER IX.

THE winter ended and spring came, and the time drew more and more near when Hilda was to go away. Her brother expected to reach England in June, and was at once to come for her: she had always known that.

The fair spring colours came upon the trees and on the distant hills: the skies were blue and sunny in those sweet spring months. Hilda used to sit at the study window, looking over the bright landscape, silent often for hours. She and Mr. Erle had taken no walks together during the winter. When the spring returned perhaps she hoped that they might walk together again, but they did not: the habit had been broken, and he never resumed it, nor had she the courage to ask him to resume it, any more. For, if she was in some respects more intimate with him now than she had been six months ago, yet she was shyer with him too: she had said many things to him then that she could not say to him now; she had been bold with him then because she had cared so slightly for him, but now she could not be bold in the old way any more.

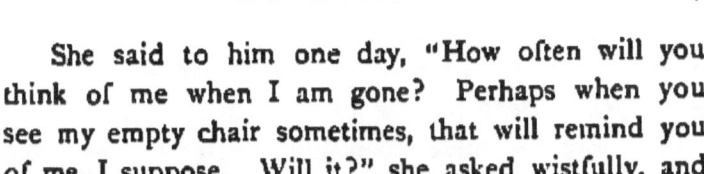

She said to him one day, "How often will you think of me when I am gone? Perhaps when you see my empty chair sometimes, that will remind you of me, I suppose. Will it?" she asked wistfully, and looked up to him with her sad eyes.

"Yes, that and many other things," he answered.

"Will there be other things?" she said. "Sometimes I think there will be nothing else than that."

And then he made no answer to her, and only after a minute's silence spoke about something else that had no connection with her last words.

He used to make her bitter many a time because he would not answer the half wistful, half reproachful, things she said. She used to try to wring answers from him that he would not speak, till she made her heart bleed. He seemed so hard and cruel to her, She told him sometimes that he was hard. She said to him indignantly once—

"I think you could see a person starving, and not give him any bread."

"I might have no bread to give him," he answered to this speech after a moment's silence.

"But you would let him starve, if you had made up your mind to do it, though you *had* bread," she retorted.

"Is that what you think of me?" he asked her.

And then, after a moment's silence—for possibly

the quiet gravity of his question checked her, and she made no answer to it—

"Suppose I gave no bread to him because the only bread I had to give had poison in it? Would my refusal to feed him be so cruel then?" he said.

Possibly she understood him when he asked her that. She looked piteously into his face for one moment, and then the colour came. She, in her hunger, would have taken bread from him (she thought), and have blessed his hand for giving it to her, though there had been poison enough in it to take her life away.

Would he go on to the end, and never tell her that he cared for her? Surely he would tell her, she cried passionately to herself; but the days went on, and he never told her. Day followed day in silence till the last of her weeks was gone, and the letter came at length that announced her brother's landing. That letter reached her one Wednesday morning. "I hope to take the night train on Thursday, so as to be with you by breakfast time on Friday," Mr. Ford wrote. "Pack your trunks, and have everything ready for starting when I come, for I shall have no time to linger, and I am impatient to have my little sister again under a roof of my own."

So here had come the end of it all! Her face went white as she opened and read her letter. She had known that it was coming, she had even expected

it that very day; yet when it came it seemed to make
the world end for her.

"They have really arrived, then? Well, that is
very delightful! And when are you to see him, my
dear?" asked tranquil Mrs. Erle.

They were having breakfast when the letter came,
and Mrs. Erle thought it was joy that made the girl
sit with her untouched meal before her, as her nervous
fingers held the paper, and her dim eyes read and
remained fastened on the few decisive lines.

"He—he will come on Friday," she answered after
a moment or two, in a low voice that had a curious
quiver in it.

She stayed in her own room that morning, crying
with bitter and hopeless tears. How could she bear
the thing that was coming to her? she sat sobbing to
herself. Unaccustomed to endurance, it seemed to
her as if her trouble was too great for her,—as if it
would overwhelm her and break her heart. How co l
she go on living, she kept crying, when she should
be separated from Michael Erle—when all that was
about her now should have passed away from her
—when the days and the weeks should come and go,
and she should never see him any more?

She did not go to the study all the morning, because she was ashamed to go with her tear-stained
face. And yet later in the day——

"Do you know why I didn't come?" she suddenly

asked Mr. Erle, with a kind of half defiance in her voice. "I didn't come, because I was crying. I have been crying because I am going away. Yes—because I am going away—and because I don't know how to bear it." And then, when she had said this, the great tears flashed into her eyes again, and she looked at him through their passionate sad brightness with a look whose anguish she thought, perhaps, he was too blunt to read.

She was standing beside him then, but they were not in his room. They had been dining, and Mrs. Erle had left the parlour after dinner, and then some question that he asked brought this speech from her. When she had made it they both stood silent for a little while, and then he spoke again; but he did not answer what she had said.

"I have been very busy all the morning," he merely told her. "Morton writes that he wants my review of Froude a day sooner than I had expected, so I shall scarcely have breathing time till I get it out of hand. I must finish it, if I can, by to-morrow night. To-day or to-morrow I shall have some extracts for you to make, if you will do them for me."

She swallowed down her tears, and asked after a moment or two, "Are they ready for me now?"

"One or two of them are ready."

"Then I had better come and do them." She said this very dejectedly.

"You can come when you like. Any time that you like, either now or to-morrow."

"I had better come now. I have nothing to do." And then she went.

"Let me do all the writing that you can these last days—will you?" she said wistfully to him presently, as she stood by his table, waiting for him to show her the marked places in the book. "Let me sit here and write for you. That isn't much to ask, is it?"

"No," he replied, very quietly.

He showed her the passages that he wanted extracted, and she sat down and began to copy them. The placid employment soothed her a little: it often soothed her only to be near him. She had said to him once, a good while ago, "I like to be with you, even when you don't speak a word to me. I think that sitting here always does me good." And now, even in her to-day's state of inward turmoil, these hours of quiet occupation comforted her, and brought her a feeling of peace. The silence round her, the summer sunshine on the floor, the motionless figure at his desk, with his busy fingers and his grave, bowed face—the sight and sense of these things tranquillized her and calmed her bitter thoughts.

She wrote for him through most of the afternoon. She said, when her work was ended—

"I felt so tired when I came up here, and now I

am not tired at all. But *you* are tired?" she added quickly after a moment.

"I have had rather a long day's work," he answered, "and I have more to do yet."

"Are you going to work to-night too?"

"Yes; I must do as much more as I can."

She sighed at that, but made no answer.

In the evening, when tea was over, she asked him if she might go back, and sit with him again.

"I only want to sit and read; I won't talk or disturb you," she said humbly.

He let her go back with him, and they spent that evening together, but almost without speaking to each other. It was June, and the days were long. She sat beside the window with a book upon her knees, reading it a little sometimes, but not reading it much, perhaps.

After the sun had gone down, in the dusk, he went to her for a few moments.

"Are you not tired with sitting so long here?" he asked her.

It was too dark to read then: she had closed her book, and the poor lips quivered as she looked up to him.

"Do you think I am tired? Am I ever tired of being here?" she replied reproachfully.

And then he said nothing for a minute, and after that, instead of answering her, he began to talk about

the beauty of the evening, and the colours that the
sunset, had left in the sky.

After only a very little while he lit his gas and
went on writing, and then presently Mrs. Erle came
in and made them go downstairs.

"You have been working the whole day long,
Michael," she said to her son. "You must be worn
out. Come down and take a little rest before you go
to bed."

She had come into the room sore, perhaps, with
a suspicion, such as she often had, that Hilda was
talking to her son, and wasting his time; but she
found the girl sitting silent enough, and Mr. Erle
busy at his desk.

"My dear, I don't think you have much light
there. It is a very bad thing for you to try your
eyes," she said to Hilda; and Hilda, hardly answering
her, rose sadly from her seat. Perhaps she had hoped
for something that she had not gained—something,
she scarcely knew what; some word from him that she
might remember before the night should end. But
now his mother had come, and he could give no such
word to her. He was talking to Mrs. Erle as he left
the room. He made way for Hilda to pass him, but
he said nothing to her as she went by.

"He has scarcely spoken to me the whole day
long. Oh, he might have talked to me a little more

—he might have been kinder to me," the poor thing thought bitterly in her wounded heart.

She said to herself when she rose next morning, "This is the last day that I shall spend with him!" The sun came in at her window as she dressed, and she felt as though she could not bear its brightness; and yet if it had not shone upon her she would have found the gloom of a sunless sky still harder to bear. Had nothing any pity for her? the poor child thought. Was nothing sorry for her? Would the world look just like this if her heart broke?

"I am coming up to do my writing now," she said to Mr. Erle, when breakfast was over; and he answered, "Very well; I shall soon be ready for you;" and they went up to the study together.

"Read for a little while until I call you," he said to her; and so she read for an hour, and then he called her and showed her what he wanted her to write.

She sat beside him all the morning. This was the last work she did for him. She said at the end of it——

"I have finished this. What shall I do next?"

And then he shook his head, and answered that he had nothing more for her to do.

"Nothing more?" she echoed wistfully, lifting up her head and looking at him with those plaintive eyes that it was often so hard for him to meet.

"No, nothing more," he said. "You have done it all now."

The dinner bell rang almost as he was speaking: perhaps he was glad to hear the sound of it. Her lip was trembling, but she rose up and did not cry. They went downstairs together, and she only spoke again when they had almost reached the parlour door.

"After tea to-night I may come and sit upstairs again—mayn't I? for the last time?" she said then.

Mrs. Erle, at the dinner-table, sat talking about her brother's coming. Mrs. Erle of late had been a little uneasy and perplexed over Hilda. "My dear, I don't think you are well," she had said to her more than once, peering at her anxiously through her spectacles; for though, as you know, she had suffered a good deal from Hilda, and the girl's presence in the house had been more of a thorn in the flesh to her than any one guessed, yet she was a kindly woman, and it had troubled her to see the young face growing less fresh and bright than it had been a year before. "I shall be so glad when her brother comes for her. The truth of it is, Michael, that she can't bear a dull life like ours," she had said sagaciously to her son. But now Mr. Ford was coming, and Mrs. Erle's heart was getting relieved and buoyant. She talked about him, and rejoiced over him to-day as they ate their dinner, till Hilda felt as if she could not bear it. How could she sit there like a hypocrite, pretending she was glad

that her brother was going to take her away, when
the thought that he was going to take her away was
breaking her heart?

"You seem to be very sure that I shall be happy
with Henry. Why, I haven't seen Henry for half-a-
dozen years. Perhaps he mayn't like me, and I mayn't
like him," she a little quenched Mrs. Erle at last by
answering sharply and petulantly. For she was so
unhappy, that she could not help being irritable, and
the poor little lip quivered a dozen times to-day with
emotions either of anger or grief.

"Are you busy still? Have you got writing to do
still—all night?" she asked Mr. Erle wistfully in the
evening. He had gone up to his room when tea was
over, and when she followed him she found him
already sitting at his desk.

He answered gently, "Yes, I have work to do. I
must get my article finished to-night."

And then, submissively and sadly, the poor child
went away to her accustomed seat. "Why will he not
talk to me? Does he not remember that it is the last
night? Will he never talk to me again?" she thought
to herself, with a great sob rising in her breast. But
yet she sat down and left him undisturbed. As she
had done last night, she took her book and sat with
it open on her knees.

Yet it was harder to-night to let the hours pass
by, and simply to sit so beside him, gaining no word

from his closed lips. Last night there still had been another night to come, but now there was *no* other night: this was the last of all, and yet he would not speak to her! As each silent minute passed that thought became more hard to bear—her heart grew sorer and sadder and more indignant. "He doesn't care for me: he doesn't care for what I suffer. It is all one to him whether I go or stay," she thought bitterly to herself. And then at last her power of endurance reached its limit. The sun had set; the twilight was coming on; and in the dusk she rose and went up to his side.

"Can't you stop writing just for a few minutes? Can't you stop for a little while, when it is the last night?" she said to him, in a half suppressed voice.

He laid his pen down as she began to speak. After a moment he answered quietly,

"Yes, I will stop if you like. But these last nights are rather hard times. Don't let us talk about this one being the last."

"Why shouldn't we talk of it?" she asked him sharply.

And then all at once, before he could answer her, she sank down on her knees, and her trembling hands went up beseechingly to him, like a child's.

"Oh, don't be hard to me, and speak as if you didn't care! Don't you see that I am breaking my heart? I don't know how to bear it! Oh, say something to me, for I don't know what to do!" she cried.

She had put her hands in his, so that he could
not do anything but take them, and her fingers clung
to him convulsively: the passionate face was looking
up to him, too, with all its poor childish love written
plain upon it. What could he do but look at it and
read it?

"It is all as hard for me as for you. If it is any
comfort to you, you may think that. But, Hilda, you
must bear my silence, for I cannot talk to you about
it," he said in a low voice.

He took her hands and held them fast together
for a moment between his own: then after that moment
he rose up, and forced her to rise with him.

"We shall not forget one another. Try to be
content with being sure of that," he said.

"But I am *not* sure of it!" she cried out.

They were standing together then: the room was
growing dusk, and she was crying. He had let her
hands go, and she was crying—desolately.

"Do you not know that I would give my life to
make you happy?" he all at once said to her; and
then he suddenly turned away. He went away to the
window, and stood there looking out.

Was he doing right? Was his course so plain
before him that the bruising of this childish heart was
part of the clear, sad duty that was laid on him? As
he stood apart from her he asked himself this question for the final time, vainly seeking for another

answer to it than the answer he had already given himself a hundred times. For only the old answer would come back with all its hard distinctness. He *was* doing right: for him there was no right thing to be done but one.

It got darker as he stood before the window. He stood there so long that the room was perceptibly in deeper twilight when he turned round again at last to look for her. She had sunk into his chair, and had laid down her head upon his desk. He turned round and saw her sitting so, and for a moment or two after he turned he could not speak to her. Then at last, "Hilda, come here to me," he said gently; and when she rose and came—for, petulant and wilful as she was, yet when he spoke to her the poor heart leapt up involuntarily to answer and obey him, and she rose and went to him like a child—he drew her hand into his arm, and stood for a little while in silence, and then—

"This year has made us friends," he said. "Do you think that I shall ever forget it? Do not reproach me or be unjust to me. We shall not be together any more, but I shall remember you; believe that."

He laid his hand gravely and almost solemnly over hers. Then there was a long pause. He had said all that he could dare to say; and she stood silent, calmed for the moment with a sweet, strange sense of peace. For it seemed to her, just for this

12*

moment, as though to part with words like these between them was something *not* so hard as death—was
something bearable, almost beautiful. He stood with
his hand on hers, and the firm, close, quiet pressure
became like some blessed balm, to draw the bitterness
from her heart.

"It is all over now," she said to herself that night
when she lay down in the dark and closed her eyes.
It was all over, and this was the end. And yet she
fell asleep, not in despair, but only like a tired child.
"He was so good to me," she said, with the tears
stealing through her shut lids; "God bless him! he
was so good."

CHAPTER X.

MR. FORD arrived next morning. He had travelled
by the night train, and. he reached the Erles' house in
time for breakfast. It was six years since he and Hilda
had met. She had been a child when they parted,
and now, when they stood face to face again, neither
of them recognized the other.

"No, I shouldn't have known you," he said, when
the first greetings were over, standing before her with
his hands upon her shoulders, and shaking his head
at her. "The old face will come back presently, I
dare say, but I suspect I might have passed you in the
street without a thought of who you were."

"And I might have passed you," Hilda replied.

She looked at her brother, but the smile with which
she answered his had little brightness in it. He seemed
like a stranger to her: the sight of him scarcely aroused
any sensation of gladness in her heart; she only
thought that to be with him, whom she did not know
—who seemed at this moment to be nothing to her—
she was to give up everything she cared for in the
world.

For it was with Hilda as it is with many another undisciplined, impulsive nature—she had delivered herself up to one desire and one emotion;
one thing had become supreme to her, and its supre-
macy had taken the flavour for her out of everything
else on earth. Hers was not a well regulated mind:
she could not care for what she wanted moderately;
she cared for what she wanted for the moment recklessly and passionately, and she cared for nothing
else.

I have been telling you a piece of the history of
such a childish, foolish woman, you know—a woman
whose character had no balance and no stability; who
went her way obedient only to the currents that for
the moment swept her hither and thither, without rule
or guidance, like a boat without a helm or rudder.
In her course through life she got amidst the rapids
sometimes; she got nearly stranded once or twice; but
those who fling themselves after her fashion on the
world at times are treated by it very tenderly, and
have their wounds bound up and healed so dexterously, that you never see the scars—while the braver
ones, who do battle with it, go often to their graves
hurt and maimed. The world, as time went on, treated
Hilda more kindly than she merited, perhaps. I told
you that at the beginning. Her suffering in this
trouble—as in other troubles afterwards—was only
a child's suffering, short and sharp. The longer,

harder, wearier pain was felt by some one else than her.

Between Mr. Ford's arrival and her final departure there was an interval of only two or three hours, and these hours were of necessity broken and unsettled. Hilda was on her feet during the greater part of them, nervously going to and fro; Mr. Ford was a good deal on his feet too, pacing the parlour up and down, and talking to whoever he could get to talk to. "My dear, can't you come in and stay quietly with your brother for a little while?" Mrs. Erle said to the girl once, meeting her wandering about the stairs in an apparently aimless manner; but she only shook her head hurriedly without speaking, and turned away. How could she go in and sit with her brother? How could she talk to him, when only to speak a common word made a lump rise in her throat?

For the end had come, and it seemed to her as if all she wanted in the world—all she could ever want —the light of her eyes, the desire of her heart, was being taken from her; as though, in so many minutes now, she should go away and leave her life behind her here. With impotent agony she flung herself upon her bed once, and lay crying that she could not bear it—that she *could* not go—she could not go! Why did he not come to her? she sobbed: he stayed with her brother, and he would not come and speak to

her. She waited for him till her heart was sick; and
the minutes passed, and he had no pity on her, for
he would not come.

"I think, Hilda," Mr. Ford said at last, calling to
her, and looking at his watch for about the twentieth
time, "I think, if you are ready, that it will be as well
to get the cab now. If you will tell me where to find
a cabstand——"

These last words were addressed to Mr. Erle, but
Mr. Erle had already risen.

"I will get a cab," he answered, and went out into
the hall, and took down his hat.

"Oh, why need *you* go?" Hilda said to him
eagerly.

She had gone into the hall too; she arrested him
as he was going out, putting her hand upon his arm,
and looking into his face with her imploring eyes.

"I shall not be away five minutes," he answered
gently.

"But then there will be no time left!"

"Mr. Erle, I should like to accompany you, if you
will allow me," said Mr. Ford, coming out suddenly
from the parlour. "There is nothing I can do for
Hilda, apparently, so we may as well go together."

She turned away without speaking again, and let
them go. Her trunks were already in the passage,
her travelling bag upon the table; there was nothing
more for her to do.

"I hope you haven't left anything, my dear," said Mrs. Erle. "It is so difficult not to forget something when one is packing. Have you got your watch on? And your nightgown, did you pack that this morning? and all your dressing things?"

"Oh yes," said Hilda impatiently.

"You have got your wraps there, I see, and your umbrella; but I don't think that strap is very secure, dear. Couldn't you draw it a little tighter?"

"It will do very well. Oh, it doesn't matter!" said poor Hilda with a break in her voice, and suddenly turned round and ran upstairs. Why did they talk to her and worry her with such foolish things? What did she care about it all? Why couldn't they leave her alone? the poor child cried.

She stood at the window in her room, trembling and sobbing, till she heard the cab drive up, and then, with one last purpose in her mind, she went back again to the hall, and stopped Mr. Erle as he came in.

"Come upstairs with me for one moment," she said to him half aloud, with feverish eagerness. "I want you to come to the study, just for the last minute!"

He made a sign of assent without replying, and they went upstairs together. They neither of them spoke till they had reached the study and gone in;

then, standing in the middle of the room, she turned round, and looked up into his face.

"I couldn't say good-bye to you downstairs," she said suddenly in her trembling voice. "I want to say good-bye to you here. You know I have been happier here than I have ever been anywhere in all my life. I shall never forget it!—never—never—never!"

He took her hands and stood before her, holding them. After a moment or two's silence he said, "God bless you!" He said "God bless you!" twice, as if that prayer was the only farewell that he dared utter. And then there was a little silence, and she burst into tears.

So quiet and tranquil the familiar room looked: his table, with the chair a little pushed aside, as he had risen from it last; her seat in the window where she had sat yesterday; the sun shining, as it had shone so often, on his books. But she was not thinking of it then; she only stood crying in the midst of it.

After a minute's silence there came a call from below, in Mrs. Erle's voice,

"Hilda, your brother is waiting for you."

"She is coming," Mr. Erle replied, answering for her, for she could not speak.

And then, a moment afterwards, "Hilda, you must go now," he said.

He held his hands out to her again (they had

fallen from her when Mrs. Erle called), but she looked
into his face with a great sob, and suddenly lifted her
own up to his neck.

"Oh, kiss me!" she said to him in a broken voice.

Then neither of them spoke again; but in the
silence he stooped down to her, and they kissed each
other with their first and last kiss.

Do you want an ending to the story? I can give
one to you quickly—in a dozen lines.

It is the summer time again of another year, and
Hilda is standing in a different kind of room from
that littered study of Michael Erle—a handsome drawing-room, richly furnished, and she is daintily dressed
in some soft white Indian stuff, and the little face is
flushed, but with something else than crying, and the
dark eyes are bright, but with something else than
tears.

"Will it really fit you, do you think?—such a tiny
thing as this,". some one is saying to her; and then
she laughs, with a half shy, happy laugh. It is only a
ring that her companion is speaking of—a hoop of
diamonds that he slips next moment (and tiny though
it is, it slips on easily) over the third finger of her left
hand.

The curtain fell on the old play a year ago. Is it

not time for the scene to shift? The tears are dried up, the anguish and the love have passed away—they belonged to yesterday; to-day knows nothing of them: they have gone to the limbo where lie the world's forgotten and discarded things.

END OF "ONLY A BUTTERFLY."

ELSPETH GRANT.

ELSPETH GRANT.

How one is haunted sometimes by a face! I remember one just now that often comes back to me
like a picture or a ghost—I can hardly tell why. It
was the face of an old woman that I first saw one
autumn day in London, five or six years ago.

I had been in the City, and it was an hour when
the City streets are crowded. As I was walking from
St. Paul's towards Temple Bar I came across her—
she was coming towards me in the midst of the busy
throng of people—a tall, gaunt, feeble old woman,
looking so utterly out of keeping with the place in
which she was; so helpless, as the passers-by roughly
hustled her from side to side; so lonely and unspeakably pathetic, with that worn, wistful, bewildered face
of hers amongst all the strong, keen faces round her,
that, though I passed her by at first, she touched me
so that I could not help turning round after a moment
or two, and going back to her. I never saw a stranger's
face that moved me more. There was something in
it, and in the utter helplessness and sadness of the

whole figure, that filled me with pity so sharp that it
was like a sudden spasm of pain.

I could not tell if she was begging, but I thought
she might be, for she was very poorly dressed, and one
of her hands was held out a little way before her; so
I took out my purse, and when I came up to her I
put something into the poor outstretched hand to attract her attention before I spoke to her, thinking that
she would turn to me: but I never saw a creature
wandering in those busy City streets so pathetically
apart from the whole of the life around her. She never
looked at me, and only with a sort of instinctive
shrinking drew in her hand, and let the money drop
down on the ground—perhaps unconsciously, perhaps
by accident, perhaps on purpose—I could not tell;
and meantime the crowd went still jostling her on,
and pushing her this way and that; and her dim old
eyes wandered over it and through it, as if they had
some far away, vague hope of finding something in it
that she had lost.

Then I spoke to her. I had picked up the money
and I did not offer it to her again. I touched her
arm, and said to her, "You are not very strong, I
think, to be alone in a place like this. Where are
you going? Do you know?"

She looked round at the sound of my voice, as if
she was startled at being addressed, and the poor old
face seemed so dreamy and astray as it gazed at me

that I scarcely thought she had understood my question; but after a moment or two, rather to my surprise, she made a sort of answer to it.

"I'm just looking for my lad," she said, in a low, half-apologetic tone that I could not much more than catch.

"Looking for him?" I repeated. "Where is he? I think you had better leave him to look after himself." But at this she made no other answer, and only began to murmur something quite inaudibly as she shook her head.

She was like some one I had loved once, and who was dead. It was that likeness that had gone to my heart at the first moment I saw her. She was so like that woman I had loved once—as that woman might have been, if she had ever grown like this one, poor, and old, and lonely—that, though I did not know what to do for her, I could not make up my mind to turn away again and leave her to herself.

"Why are you looking for your son? Where has he gone?" I said to her once more.

"Where has he gane? Eh, I dinna ken that," she said. "That's what I'm aye thinkin' on."

"But do you mean that you are just wandering about here, hoping to find him?" I asked. "Oh, my poor woman, there is little use in that! How long is it since you saw him last?"

She turned her sad old eyes to me with such a

look in them—as sad and wild a look of pain as I ever saw in any human face.

"How lang is it?" she said. "Oh, hone!—he's been awa' these thirty years!"

We were standing in the sunshine, with the crowds of busy people passing us, and the black, big dome of St. Paul's looming out against the sky. The great clock, after those last words of hers, began to strike twelve, and people as they hurried on glanced at their watches. What a breathless world it was for most of *them*—and here was one woman whose life had stood still for thirty years!

There was an empty doorway near us, and I drew her into it, and then asked her where she lived. She told me at Chelsea, and that she had walked all the way into the City that morning. "No that I had ony hope o' findin' him; but there are aye whiles when I canna rest," she said. She seemed to haye had no special intention of coming here rather than elsewhere; she had merely wandered aimlessly on: she scarcely seemed even to know now where she was.

"And have you no one to take care of you?" I asked her.

"Na, na," she said; "I never had a dochter, and my man's been deid these sixteen year. I thought my lad wad ha' come hame when his father was deid; but maybe he didna ken,—and he was aye frighted o' his father. Eh, my laddie!" she cried, and gave a sudden bitter wail, that died away in the sound of the roar all round us.

It was perhaps a needless thing to do—I got laughed at for it afterwards—but I took her home. I had not the heart to leave the desolate old woman there in the street alone. Besides, her way lay for several miles in the same direction as mine, so it was easy to take her with me. She gave me an address of a house in a small respectable street in Chelsea, where she had a room, she said; and when we reached the place I went to her room with her, and found it very clean, though poor and bare enough. The house was kept by a bustling-looking woman, who came to me before I went away, and showed herself very ready to talk of her troubles with her lodger. "She's as decent and respectable an old body as ever stepped within a door," she said to me; "but, bless you, she's not to be trusted to herself, not when these fits is on her. She'll go wandering away some day, I always tell her, and nobody will never see her any more. But she's not right in the head, poor dear! that's it. She's not been right never since she lost her son. We was neighbours then—for both she and I, we've lived about here these five-and-thirty years; and from the time he went away she was never the same woman again. Well, yes; it was a bad story, ma'am. Jim Grant, he was a hard man, as hard a man as ever

13*

you saw; and the boy wasn't good for much, I think.
Of course his mother was fond of him, and he was
fond of her, poor fellow, I'll say that for him; but he
was a foolish, idle lad, and he fell into bad company,
and drove his father near mad. He couldn't stand it
at all. He was an honest, hard-working man, and he
couldn't stand it. The two, they came to words together first, and then they came to blows; and I
remember yet, as well as if it was yesterday, the night
at last when his mother came running in to me like a
wild woman, and calling to my husband to go and
part them. Poor thing! that was the end of it all.
The boy was gone before my husband got to the
house, and he never set foot within its doors again."

This was most of what I heard about Elspeth
Grant that first day; but she had interested me with a
strong interest, and I went back often afterwards, and
saw her again. It was a curious case. I found that
she was often so quiet and composed that you might
sit for a long time and talk with her, and never
suspect that she had any trouble that had unhinged
her mind; except that to me there was always an in-
describably pathetic expression in her eyes, like the
appealing look of a dumb animal. It never left them;
I never saw her without it; it was one of the saddest,
most wistful looks I ever beheld in any face.

She was not in general given to talk much about
her son,—her Scotch reserve and pride, I think,

generally keeping her from doing that, unless she was very sure of sympathy,—except at those times when her fits of restlessness came on, and then she would wander out to look for him, and would tell her sorrow to any one who questioned her. But these were the times when she was "not herself," as her landlady put it. She often was thoroughly herself, and then the proud old woman was very slow to seek for sympathy, and very cautious in accepting it. It was always very touching to me to see how conscious she was of her want of sanity during those restless attacks of hers, and yet how she shrank from acknowledging it, or speaking of them.

"I was aye a gude walker," she said to me, the first time I went back to see her, trying wistfully to give some appearance of reason to the circumstances under which I had come across her—"I was aye a gude walker, and the City's a gran' place. I gang there noo and again, just for a ploy. Ye'll ha' been in St. Paul's, noo, yersel, mony a time, I guess?" she said, beginning to divert my attention from asking painful questions of her by starting a quite irrelevant question of her own.

Though she was on her guard with me, however, at the first, it was not long before she began to trust me enough to tell me her story with her own lips, and I have sat often with her listening to that history of her life—with its joys that had ceased, and its sorrows that had *never* ceased—as one listens to an old story of people dead and gone, yet knowing while you listen that to the voice that speaks to you these past and vanished things are the only things that seem to have reality and life. I always felt this with her: she was always to me like a woman whose life had stopped for thirty years, and who was waiting for it to begin again, and with a strange fixed belief that it *would* begin sooner or later. For she never believed that that son of hers—her "bairn," as she always called him—was dead; she never spoke of him as if he *could* be dead. She would go over all the reasons that could have kept him from her so long, and never speak of death as one of them; and if *you* spoke of it she would not listen to you. "He's no deid!" she would cry. "Eh, if he was deid, do ye think I wadna ken?" Her whole life had so grown into a passionate love and waiting for him that she could not believe him other than alive; she could not even believe him changed; in the sight of those poor eyes of hers he had remained for thirty years the boy who had loved her, and who had left her before he had grown into a man.

She was seventy-six, she told me once; that was when I knew her first. She was very poor, but her husband had been a saving man, and had left her a little, and she knitted stockings, and so contrived to make both ends meet. She had no one near her who

belonged to her. I asked her once if she never felt
any desire to go back to her own people in Scotland,
but she answered me with almost a look of reproach.
"Wad ye hae me gang awa', and no be here when
my bairn comes hame?" she cried. Yet if her heart
was warm towards anything except her son, it was
warm towards the land of her birth, and sometimes
for an hour or two I would get her to tell old Scotch
stories to me, forcing her for the moment to forget
her grief, and move out of the shadow of that partial
insanity that was always more or less brooding over
her.

For two years, off and on, sometimes pretty fre-
quently, I used to go to see her; then at the end of
that time she fell ill. She had been getting more
and more feeble through the winter, and at last early
in the spring she ceased to rise from her bed. "We
shall not have her, I'm thinking, when another winter
comes round," her landlady said to me; and I thought
so too; but yet it was strange now, ill though
she was, and with death, as one would think even she
herself must be aware, coming near her, she still clung
to the passionate belief of so many years—that she
should see her son before she died. To the rest of
us her hope seemed a mere dream, but to her it was
the one reality left on earth.

I used to go to her during the last weeks that she

lived as often as I could, for she was very lonely, and
was always glad when I came to sit beside her and
read to her. For many a year—perhaps, for what I
knew, all her life—she had had no book in her possession except her Bible, and it had been used by her
till some of its pages were worn thin. I used to read
it to her now by the hour together, and she would
often follow whole chapters with the movement of her
lips, not saying them after me, but with me, as she
remembered them. One evening there was a certain
Psalm that I read to her, and as I read it I saw the
tears rolling down her cheeks. "My lad read yon to
me the night before he went awa'," she said, when I
had ended. And then she suddenly lifted up her
hands in the bed with a great wail. "Oh, my bairn,"
she cried, "when are you coming hame?"

It was one evening in the spring. Her room was
on the ground-floor—a little room facing the street.
She often had the door open, and the street door was
often open too. She never seemed to mind the noise.
There were children in the house who used to run in
and out, and the landlady's voice—for she was a stir-
ring kind of woman—not unfrequently drowned mine.
I remember while I read that Psalm to-day—it was
the one which tells us that those who sow in tears
shall reap in joy—I had hardly been able to hear the
words I said; yet they had reached the ears that lay
listening for them, and had brought back the sound

to her of that other voice that had spoken them two-
and-thirty years ago.

After she had given that bitter cry I closed the
book for a little, and sat still. I sat thinking—first of
her, and then of other things, I suppose; and the lids
had dropped over her eyes, and I thought she had
begun to doze, as she often did now from weakness.
We had both remained quietly so for about ten minutes, when all of a sudden she gave a sharp movement that made me start, and with an excited face
struggled to raise herself in bed.

"Wha's that?" she cried. "There's somebody oot
by. Dinna ye hear? dinna ye hear? Oh! my bairn,—
my bairn!" she all at once screamed wildly, and weak
as she was, she lifted herself up, and sat gaunt and
white, with her eyes upon the door.

I supposed for a moment that she had been frightened by a dream, and, startled though I was—for
there had been something strangely eerie in the shrill-
ness and wildness of that sudden cry—my first im-
pulse was to try and soothe her: but I had hardly
opened my lips to speak when the words upon them
died away, for through the open doorway I saw some
one come into the room. It was a tall, rough-looking,
red-bearded man. He stood at the door for a moment; and then, with an air half of unwillingness and
hesitation, came in, and walked up to the bed where
the old woman was still sitting upright, but with the

arms that had been so passionately stretched out at
first, suddenly all drawn back and pressed against her
bosom; and on the face—the old, worn, pitiful, pathetic face—God help her!—such a look!

He went up to the bedside, and, with only a moment's silence, said bluntly to her,

"You'll hardly know me, mother." And then he
touched her—I think he put his hand upon her
shoulder. He would have bent down and kissed her,
perhaps, if she had not held him suddenly back from
her at arm's length.

"Wha are ye? Ye are no my bairn!" she cried in
her shrill shrieking voice. She was trembling. I saw
the thin, feeble fingers quiver as she tried to grasp his
coat.

"If I'm not, I don't know who is then," he answered, with a half bitter laugh. "What! I'm so
changed as all that—am I, mother? Why, I remember
you!" the man said suddenly, with a kind of jar in
his voice, and looked at her, perhaps—I could not tell
—with the eyes that had looked at her when he was
young.

And then, I suppose, she knew him. But I hardly
know what followed next for a few moments, till I
saw her arms about him, and heard her sobbing over
him, half in the agony of her disappointment, half in
the great flood of her joy, with sobs as if the worn-
out heart would break.

So he had come back; but he had come as,
throughout all her long years of patient waiting, she
had never dreamed that he would come. Her son
still, yet so changed from all that he had ever been
to her of old, that she looked on him with a kind of
dumb, strange awe, and followed him with eyes filled
with half frightened, half inquiring wonder. He was
a rude, blunt, surly sort of fellow, and yet not without
a rough kind of tenderness in him. He had been
part of his life a sailor, and part of it little better
than a tramp. He had been in London at times, and
once or twice, he told me, he had come out here to
look at the old place. But he had never come since
his father's death, and he had never known whether
his father was dead or not. What was the use of his
troubling them? he said. He had been trouble enough
to his mother when he was young. He was out of
employment now, and had just come, he said, "to try
to get a look of the old woman's face."

It was, as I say, only a rude sort of tenderness
that was in him; but yet he was kind to that poor old
mother during the week or two longer that she lived.
He would often sit by her bedside and talk to her;
the two would talk together about a thousand things
that had happened in the old time. She would sometimes hold his hand, looking wonderingly at the coarse,
rough fingers. Often for hours she would lie watching
him and looking in his face.

I do not know if she was happy; I never asked her. The thing she had desired so long had come to her; but it had come under a guise so strange that she hardly any longer knew it. The prayer she had prayed for thirty years was granted to her; she had nothing left to ask. The occupation, the suffering, the hope of life were all gone. Perhaps she was happy; but her face, after her son came home, had always to me a sort of bewilderment in it; it was almost as if, now she had found the thing that she had sought so long, she had lost something else that she should *never* find again.

Or at least, if she ever found it, it was only for one last golden moment before she died. I knew that it was very near the end, one April day when I came in to see her. She was lying, looking very weak —half sleeping, I thought. I sat for a little while by her bedside; then she began to move. "Laddie, are you there?" she said, and stretched her hand out with a half blind movement. He came to her and took it, and she began to murmur something almost inaudibly —something about our having put out the light.

I hardly know how the thought came to me, but when we had spoken to her once or twice, and she had not seemed to hear us, it struck me that the sound of some familiar words might still pierce the ears that were fast becoming dulled to earthly voices,

and I opened her Bible at that Psalm that I had read
the night her son came home, and told him to read
it to her. As he read, after a few moments I saw that
she was listening; the weary look in her face changed
into something soft, bright, contented. "Bairn," she
said, when he had finished, "ye aye read that weel."

He was not a man who was often or quickly
moved; but a minute after this he was kneeling by
the bedside, with his face hidden upon the clothes,
and her dying fingers had touched and were wandering about his hair. She began to murmur words that
I could hardly hear. Only now and then I caught
some broken sentence, enough to tell me that all the
present had faded from her, and that this last hour of
all her earthly hours had made her son, for her, a
child again. She was stroking the locks that had been
curled and golden once—she was dreaming that the
world had gone back for thirty years. "Bairn, only
be gude," I heard the feeble voice say once, "and
ye'll make yer mother's heart sing wi' joy."

These were the last words I heard her utter. She
fell presently into a quiet sleep, and so passed away.
When all was over the face looked smiling and calm,
as I had hardly ever seen it look in life. She had
borne her burden, and gone to her rest.

This was all her story. Many another woman has
had much the same sort of one; but somehow, to this

day, I can never pass the place where I first saw Elspeth Grant, but the thought of her history comes back to me, and the memory of her pathetic figure comes back, with a pity too great for words.

END OF "ELSPETH GRANT."

LOST AT SEA.

LOST AT SEA.

There he lay in the sunshine, a great black, noble animal, with his work in this world done. I was standing at his side looking at him when my friend came up and joined me.

"Are you trying to make friends with our old Brutus?" he said to me. "Ah, he doesn't care much for making new friends now. He would only like to find the *old* friends again that he buried long ago in that mysterious past of his."

My friend stooped as he spoke, and stroked the great soft head. "Poor Brutus!" he said, "poor old faithful dog!"

It was not much of a story, yet it was rather curious. About five years ago my friend and his family were staying during the summer at a little sea-side town on the north coast of France. It was a quiet and rather dull place, except that its harbor was always lively with the coming and going of fishing-boats and collier brigs, and such-like craft, the watching of which was quite an endless delight to the

children, who, indeed, spent every moment they
could steal from morning to night down at the quay,
staring with all their might, and as often as they
could doing more than staring, at all that went on
there.

It was a fine great open sea, that even in summer
was pretty rough at times, coming tumbling often in
great waves over the beach, and covering all the pier
with showers of spray. Charlie and Willie were always in a state of huge delight whenever those big
waves came rolling landward. They used every
morning, as soon as they were out of bed, to run
to their bedroom window, with little shoeless feet and
bare legs, to see whether the white crests were there.

Of course they never thought of anything — for
they were very small creatures—but of the fun that it
was to see the leaping and rolling water, and of the
delight of being sent scampering up the beach when
some bigger wave than all the rest would run after
them as it broke upon the sands, as if it were resolved to catch them and wet their stockings and
shoes at least, let their little legs fly as fast as they
would. "It must be rough weather at sea," their father
and mother used to say sometimes in their hearing,
especially during one week, when the north wind blew
with a strange, wild roaring, and down about the pier
the fishermen stood looking through their glasses out
to sea, anxiously shaking their heads now and then;

but Willie and Charlie only grew merrier as the
wind blew stronger; they thought that to be out
upon the beach when they could not keep their
footing, and when the very air was white with spray
was the finest fun that they had ever had in all their
lives.

"I wish it would blow like this forever!" Charlie
would say.

And then Willie, who was the youngest, and who
never liked to be outdone, would cap Charlie's speech,
and cry with enthusiasm, "I wish it would blow ten
times harder!"

(For they were a pair of little geese, you know;
but then it is only in the nature of things that children
should be geese; and indeed, for my own part, I don't
think I should be inclined to like *any* young creatures
much who talked at ten as if they had the sense of
twenty.)

Well, it had been rough weather for near a week,
and then soft south breezes came back, and the wild
waves calmed themselves, and the fishing-boats that
for several days had been doing almost no work put
out again to sea. There was a great deal going on in
the harbor after the wind went down, and Charlie and
Willie, watching it, were as happy as the day was long.
One morning they were in the midst of it all as usual,
pushing their prying little feet and faces everywhere,
getting a good-natured fisherman now to take them

14*

for half an hour in his boat, now playing about the
masts and rigging of the little brigs, and gabbling
away in their broken French to the sailors, many of
whom by this time knew the two lads and were kind
to them.

It was a bright, warm summer day, with just wind
enough to make a little curl upon the waves, and to
fill the sails as the fishing-boats put out. There were
vessels coming in this morning as well as leaving the
harbor. Several brigs that had been expected for
some days, and that the storm had delayed, got into
port to-day. But there was one especially that amongst
all the rest attracted the boys' attention. It was an
English collier, standing on whose deck, as she came
near, they saw a great black, noble Newfoundland dog.
The creature was standing upon his four feet, taking
no notice of any one, but slowly moved his head from
side to side, as if he was vainly looking for something
that he could not find,—standing quite still, so pas-
sive that even when the boat touched the quay, and
people came up and stroked and spoke to him, he
merely let them do it, and never moved so much as
the tip of his tail in answer to them.

The children had caught sight of him with a shout
of delight. "O, see what a big dog!" Willie had
cried, and, clapping their joyful little hands, they
started forward to get as near to the brig as they
could. They saw several people gather round the

creature presently, and upon that they pushed their
way into the boat too, squeezing in cleverly between
the sailors' legs, till they got quite close to where the
dog was, with the master of the brig standing by his
side, and telling this sad little story:—

In the gray of the summer morning, he was saying, almost as the French coast was coming into
sight, one of the crew of the brig had seen a little
black speck dancing on the water far away. They
could not tell what it was,—it was too indistinct for
that,—but they knew it might be a drowning man; so
they lowered their little boat at once, and made for
him as hard as they could pull. But it was no man.
When they came near they found nothing but this
poor lost dog, floating on a bit of wreck, the spar of
some vessel that had probably foundered in the storm,
and gone silently down with all her crew. They took
him into their boat and brought him back with them.
This was all his story.

Here he stood now,—dazed, half-starved, bewildered, looking with strange eyes at each strange face
about him,—dumb through it all. As the master of
the collier told the little story, more than one pitying
hand was put forward to stroke the big black head;
but the creature took no notice of any one of them,
only stood quite still, piercing through the little group
with those sad, eager, human eyes of his. "Poor
fellow! Poor dog!" they said.

The children stood a little from him with grave, touched faces. They were gazing so earnestly at him that they did not see their father, who had come down to the quay—as he came often—to give a momentary eye to his young monkeys, and see that they were not drowning themselves or getting into any other hopeless mischief, and who was standing now behind them, and had been listening while the master told his tale. They only knew that he was there when they suddenly heard his voice.

"What are you going to do with him? Will you part with him?" he called out to the master. Then the lads turned round with a little cry. "O father!" they exclaimed; and their hearts leaped to their mouths. They were afraid to say anything more,—afraid to utter another word; they stood with their lips parted with eagerness as they waited for the master's answer.

"Well, sir, I'm open to an offer for him," the man said, after a moment's silence, and then the children burst into a shout of delight.

Ten minutes afterwards they were walking home with the noble beast between them. They chattered away as they went of all that they would do with him, what they should call him, how he should go everywhere with them, how many things they would teach him; they held him by the ear, and stroked his head, and clapped his back, and gambolled round him. Who can tell what *his* thoughts were all the time? Who could tell them, as he walked on with those dumb, wondering, patient eyes of his, with the new faces round him, and the new voices in his ears, and all the *old* world and the *old* life gone from him like a dream?

"We brought him home with us in a week or two," my friend said to me (we had been walking up and down the lawn while he told me the little story), "and the boys soon grew very fond of him; but it is a curious thing that, during all these five years he has been with us now, he has never grown more than half at home here. I think he has been as happy with us as he would have been anywhere, and a more docile, patient, kindly natured beast than he is you never knew; but yet he has always to me been like a dog living with a broken heart. I don't believe for my part that he has ever forgotten that old master of his, whoever he may have been, for a day or an hour since he lost him. Look at him now. Look what a fine human pathos there is about that tragic, silent face of his. Depend upon it he is thinking of the old story at this moment, puzzling it all out again, remembering, perhaps, how he saw the boat go down, and heard his master's last cry,—if, indeed, it *was* his last. Perhaps he may doubt even yet whether it was. I sometimes think he has still at moments a kind of forlorn hope that the lost days will come back again, and the lost eyes look into his once more."

We went up to him again where he lay, and stood

looking at him. He was dozing, with eyes half closed
in the sunshine, his black coat grown a little rusty
now, his ears drooping, his senses, perhaps, beginning
to be dulled by age, for he was old; he was not likely
to live very much longer, my friend said.

As we stood so he took no notice of us; he was
thinking of other things,—perhaps in a half-waking
dream living the old life again. "Poor Brutus!" I
said once, and stooped down to smooth his grand old
head, but still he did not move or look up.

"Ah, he doesn't care for that name," my friend said.
"He will answer to it sometimes, but he knows very well
that he had another name once quite different from
'Brutus.' We have never been able to find out what it
was; *it* is buried, too, with all the rest of his history."

We heard the boy's voices coming towards us
merrily, and their footsteps on the gravel under the
chestnut-trees. For a moment Brutus opened his
eyes at the sound of them, and gently moved his
bushy tail; then, stretching out his great fore-paws
with a peaceful sigh, he laid his head down on them
and dozed again. We left him lying so, slumbering
calmly in the sunshine, with his doggish, faithful
thoughts, perhaps, gone dreamily back to the old days,
and hearing in sleep the old voices that were lost to
him forever in that sorrowful night when the unknown
ship went down at sea.

END OF "LOST AT SEA."

THE OLD LIFE-BOAT.

THE OLD LIFE-BOAT.

A TRUE STORY.

"WHAT an ugly old boat!" Fred said, and kicked it with his foot.

It *was* an ugly old boat, as it lay on the beach in the golden sunshine, patched all over, seamed, and battered; a great lumbering hulk of a thing, looking quite out of place, both Fred and Matty thought, amongst all the other bright, dapper little boats that surrounded it, or rode out on the blue sea. Fred felt as if he could not express sufficient contempt for it in any other way than by kicking it; so he kicked it once, and then he kicked it again, while Sister Matty stood by and looked at him quite approvingly.

"I never saw such an ugly old boat in all my life!" said Fred.

"I wonder they don't break it up or burn it," said Matty, contemptuously.

"Nay, I wonder how they could ever have built it at all!" cried Fred; and his feelings were so much roused now that he kicked it a third time.

"Fred!" suddenly called a sharp, clear voice across

the sands; and Fred looked up, not quite easy in his
mind, for he knew the voice very well, and he knew a
certain warning tone in it, too, which, on many various
occasions in the course of his career (he was just
seven, and Matty was a year and a half older), had
disturbed him at the moments when he was especially
enjoying himself. So he looked up, and shouted out
"Yes!" in answer; then (though, for his own part, he
could not see a vestige of harm in what he was doing),
reflecting that it was best to be prudent,—for Fred
had learned by sad experience that you hardly ever
can tell when you are not getting into mischief in this
world,—he stood still, and abstained from kicking the
old boat any more.

The lady who had called to him came quickly
forward across the sands; and as soon as she was
near enough to speak with ease, "Fred," she said, "if
you kick that old boat, and try to break in its sides,
you will deserve that somebody should kick you."

"But it's so ugly!" said Fred, a little doggedly.

"Is that any reason for kicking it? You are no
beauty yourself," said the lady.

"I'm not as ugly as *it* is!" cried Fred, indignantly;
and he felt so much hurt by the implied comparison
that for a moment he instinctively raised his toes
again; but luckily he recollected himself in time, and
resumed his footing.

"If there were any chance, Fred, that you would

do as much good in your day as this old boat has
done,—that you would live as noble a life, and have
as many lips to bless your name when you are old,—
I for one would be content to have you, not only as
ugly as it is now, but ten times uglier."

"Oh mother, what do you mean?" cried Matty;
and both the children stood and stared at her.

"Do you want to know what I mean? Well, sit
down here, then, and I'll tell you. Sit in the shadow
of the old boat, if you like, and I'll tell you one of
the noble things—the first noble thing—that it ever
did."

The children sat down, and she began to talk to
them. She sat leaning against the old boat's side.
The sparkling yellow sands stretched out all round
them, and beyond the sands was the blue, sunny sea,
with just a delicate little changing line of foam at its
edge as it broke in bright, tiny waves upon the shore.
Those waves were dancing a little wilder and more
quickly on one side, where the rough, strong pier
stretched out amongst the rocks; and the children's
eyes turned oftenest to watch them here, leaping up
with sudden, light, airy springs, and tumbling this
way and that, as if they were half in play and half
in anger.

"I wish there would come a real good storm, with
waves like mountains," Fred had said to Matty, only
half an hour ago; and Matty had replied cheerily, that

she hoped one *would* come before they went home again, and that it would be a shame, indeed, if it didn't; for Fred and Matty did not live at this seaside town,—which, in fact, they had never seen, until two days before, though it had been their mother's birthplace,—but had another home somewhere else, many miles away.

"You can't imagine, children," said the lady, "from what you see now, how wild this coast looks on many a winter day. If you were here then, you would often find that you could hardly keep your footing out on these open sands; and, far off as the sea looks, yet even at this distance the spray from it would come upon your faces, and, if you went near to it, it would almost blind you. Round there where the rocks are, if you once saw the great winter waves rolling, you would never forget them."

"I wish it was winter now!" cried Fred, eagerly. "I should like to see them."

"*I* have seen them often," said the lady,—"oftener than I ever wish to see them again; for it is a terrible sight, though a grand one too, and sometimes a very, very sad one. Do you know how many a ship has struck out there on those rocks, Fred, and how many a life has been lost upon them?"

"No," said Fred, a little awe-struck, and looking in her face.

"There have been more wrecks than you would

like to think of; and if there are fewer now, and
fewer lives lost, it is all owing to this noble old boat,
and to the brave men who have manned her."

"Oh, mother, is she a life-boat, then?" Matty said,
and her eyes brightened.

"Yes, she is a life-boat; and I remember long
ago, when I was a little girl, sitting just as we are
doing now by her side, and hearing my mother tell
me of the first night that she put out to sea.

"It was a wild October night. All the town had
long gone to bed, and the wind had been roaring and
raving for many hours, when very early in the morning, a good while before the dawn, hundreds of people
were awakened by the sudden booming of a gun at
sea. It was a minute-gun,—a signal from a ship in
distress, as almost everybody who heard it knew.
Men, and women too, sprang out of their beds, dressed
themselves, and hurried down to the beach through
the great driving wind. They knew from the near
sound of the gun that the vessel must be close in
shore, and very soon through the darkness they saw
the lights at her mast-head. She had struck on those
rocks that you see out there, where the waves are
dancing and playing so lightly. They were dancing
in another kind of way that night.

"When a ship went on the rocks in a storm like
this, there had till now been very little that any one
could do for her. Brave men were always at hand

(for in all the world, children, there are no braver men than you may find in almost every seaport town or fishing village), ready to go out, when it was possible, through the surf, and try to throw ropes to the poor perishing people, and so to save a few lives now and then. But sometimes, when the sea was very high, nothing of this kind was possible, and then there was nothing for it but to stand still with aching hearts, and watch the wrecked ship breaking up, as far as it was possible to watch it in the darkness, or through the blinding spray, and listen helplessly to the sad cries that sometimes reached the shore even above the wildest roaring of the storm. But to-night something was to be tried that had never been tried yet.

"Not long before, a few gentlemen of the town, headed by one whose name— Well, never mind his name just now," the lady said, interrupting herself with a half-smile; "we will merely at present call him the Master; for at this time in everything that was done he *was* the master. These gentlemen had met together, and decided that they would subscribe amongst themselves for a life-boat. So the boat had been built, had been in its place for a month or two, and the fishermen had gravely shaken their heads over it. It was a queer, new-fangled-looking sort of thing, they said to one another. And they had looked very doubtfully at the Master when he talked to them, and tried to make them understand how a boat that was built like this life-boat of his, all cased and lined with cork to make it buoyant, might put out safely on a sea in which their ordinary small craft could never live. The Master talked very well, and had a shrewd tongue of his own, they said; but he was only a landsman; what could *he* know about the sea?

"Now, as they crowded down upon the beach, every man of them was wondering what the Master meant to do. He soon left them in no doubt as to that. Hardly ten minutes had passed since the first gun had been fired, when he was at the boat-house, unlocking the door.

"A little knot of men were gathered round him, some of whom had followed him out of curiosity, and a few of them, perhaps, because they were ready to trust him. He threw the doors wide open.

"'She's all ready. We'll have her down in a couple of minutes,' he cried.

"It was *he* who had taken care beforehand that she should be ready. He didn't lose a moment.

"'Here, lads! Throw these chains across your shoulders,' he called aloud. 'She'll run as fast as you can go with her. Steady now! steady! All's right!'

"They had only to draw her by her chains (you shall see, some day, children, the sort of bed on which she lies), and she ran forward on her two great wheels, like a carriage. In little more than the two minutes those wheels were crunching down the soft sand of the beach.

"A few of the people there set up a shout as the boat came in sight, but the greater number of them held their tongues, and only stood and shook their heads again, as they had been doing any time for the last six weeks.

"'We're none of us cowards, that I know of, but the Master's like to find himself mistaken, if he thinks to get a crew for his fancy boat on such a night as this,' one man said to a little knot of others that were standing with him; and there was not one of them but seemed to think as he did.

"'I wouldn't go out in her for ten pound,' one said.

"'She'll be swamped before ever they can launch her,' cried another.

"For it was indeed a fearful night, wild enough to make the bravest there grow grave at the thought of putting out to sea, even in the strongest boat that ever hands built. And yet, wild as it was, the Master went straight on with his work, as if he hardly knew that the wind was blowing, or the sea flinging its surf into his face.

"They brought the boat down almost to the water's edge, and then the men who had been drawing her stood still. The Master stood still too, and looked about him. It was dark night yet, you know; he couldn't see much; he stood with his back to the white boat, and with the light of a lantern that some one held falling full upon him. Everybody could see *him*, and he was *worth* seeing, children, for in all the town there was no nobler-looking man,—but he for his part could only see a dim mass of faces pressing near him,—eager and anxious faces, all curious to know what he would say or do.

"'Now, my lads, who will go with her?' he called out loud.

"Then he turned from one side to the other; but no one answered him. There was a little movement in the crowd, but that was all; no one seemed ready to be the first to speak.

"The Master looked sharp round him, and spoke again.

"'I didn't think you would have let me ask twice. What! is no one willing? You, John Martin,'—and he pointed suddenly at one man whose face he saw, —'will you come?'

"In an instant the crowd made a clear way for the man who had been singled out to pass through it; but he merely came forward a step or two, and as though he only did it because he was ashamed.

"All at once a voice not far from the Master began to speak in a grumbling, discontented way.

"'It's easy for them as stay at home themselves

15*

to call on poor fellows like us to throw away our lives.'

"The Master flashed round with his quick, bright eyes. He could not see who had spoken, for it was all dark in the direction whence the voice had come; but he looked straight that way.

"'Do you think I ask any of you to risk what I am not going to risk myself?' he cried, in such a voice that everybody seemed to hear him through all the noise of the waves. 'Whoever may be second, I'll be the first man to step into her. Now, who will come next?'

"They gave him a cheer all at once, and two or three voices called out 'Shame!' to the man who had spoken in the dark. Then, the next instant, John Martin was at his side.

"'I'll be the next, Master,' he said. And from that moment, one after another, they pressed forward,— they were such really brave men, though they had held back for a few seconds at the first. In two or three minutes the Master might have manned his boat twice over. It was not, probably, that they believed in what it could do a bit more than they had done for weeks past, but something had been roused in them by his words. The same feeling which has made all generous-hearted men who have ever lived or ever will live in this world ready for similar risk made them ready at his asking to face danger and death.

"So they launched the boat. That was no easy matter to do, but they did it safely; and in a few moments all that the crowd on shore could see was the little white spot she made, tossed up and down, and here and there, on the dark, wild waves.

"She had not far to go, but it must have been a hard voyage, children; and I think the Master had need indeed to be a brave man, sailing, as he did, with a crew that had no confidence in his power to lead them, but had followed him only because for the moment their hearts were fired by his own courage. Perhaps, when it was too late, some of them might have repented, and wished that they had their feet on dry land again. Perhaps, as they fought their wild way on, which must have seemed such a hopeless way to most of them, some might even have reproached him for having tempted them to leave their wives to become widows and their children fatherless. At any rate, some of those poor wives on shore spoke out like this, crying, and wringing their hands. For the most part the women had been slower to reach the beach than the men, and several who had husbands amongst those that had sailed in the life-boat only learned where they had gone when the boat had been out for half her time at sea. When they did learn it, they were wild with terror, and stood wailing and

crying like broken-hearted creatures, for they thought
that they should never look on their husbands' faces
any more.

"The boat was out for, perhaps, half an hour,—a
long half-hour! Can you fancy how the crowd of
people watched her from the shore? Again and again
they lost sight of her, and thought that she had gone
down; but again and again the white, bright spot
gleamed upon the waves, like a star of hope to those
who were watching her with strained eyes and beating
hearts. They shouted when she rose, cheering her on
with cries that she could not hear; and when she
sank and disappeared they gasped for breath, and
could not speak to one another. And then, presently,
the pale gray dawn slowly began to break.

"It was half twilight when the life-boat came back
to land, with her work done. They could see her
more plainly then, coming slowly, tossed and beaten
wildly, yet still battling her brave way on, minute after
minute bringing her nearer home. They flocked down
to the water's edge—and beyond it—to meet her,
some of them entering the very surf where they could
scarcely stand, that they might be the first to lay their
hands upon her, the noble boat! and drag her through
to the safe sands. As they reached her, what a shout
they gave! and as one by one her crew sprang out,—
the men who had sailed in her, and the men whom
she had saved,—how they caught and wrung them by

the hands, as if they had all been friends alike! The wreck was a foreign fishing-smack, and they had brought off every man on board.

"The Master had been the first to set his foot within the boat, and he was the last to leave her. He stood up, waiting till his time came, in the pale half-light; and against the gray morning sky, they all saw him, and broke suddenly into a cheer that was like a blessing from many hundred lips. They gathered about him as he jumped on shore. He had been right, and they wrong, they said. Even the poor crying women, who had been saying such bitter things of him five minutes before, came round him now with their eyes wet with another kind of tears.

"The old boat has been out since that night, children, in many another wild sea. See how she has got patched all over, how worn and battered she is! But her scars are all noble, like a soldier's wounds; for every one of them she can count a life that she has saved. Would you like her better now, Fred, do you think, if she were spruce and bright and new? Will you ever have the heart again to lay a rough touch on her worn old sides?"

Fred hung his head a little abashed, and the lady sat silent for a moment or two; then, looking up again, she went on speaking:—

"But, old as she is, she is not past work even yet; though all those who sailed in her that first night have finished *their* work long ago, and most of their names even are forgotten now. Amongst them all there is only one name that is remembered still, but *that* will be remembered as long as the old boat herself lives. When that night was over, in gratitude to the Master, and in memory of what he had done, they called her by his name. The old letters are there still where they were painted; go round and read them."

The children found where the name was written in dim, dark letters; but the first word was a long one, and Fred knit his brows in deep perplexity over it. Matty, however, who could read better than Fred, began to spell it out.

"C-h-r-i-s, Chris," spelt Matty, "t-o, to—" And then Matty's face lighted up suddenly into a look of bright surprise. "'Christopher Douglas'!" cried Matty. "Why, that's grandpapa's name!"

And then the lady looked round and laughed.

"Yes, it is grandpapa's name, and it was grandpapa's father's name before him. And for my own part, children, I think the noblest record of his life that your great-grandfather has left behind him are those dim letters on the old life-boat."

END OF "THE OLD LIFE-BOAT."

WAS ELIZABETH RIGHT?

WAS ELIZABETH RIGHT?

———

MANY people whom I have heard speak of Elizabeth Riviere have said, with more or less of decision,
that she was right; others, with more or less of vehe-
mence, that she was wrong. The question is one
that, whether in her case or in other similar cases,
will never be conclusively settled: but I will tell you
her story, and leave you to judge of her conduct for
yourselves.

Elizabeth Riviere's father and mother lived far
away from town, in a large rambling house in one of
the northern counties. They were wealthy people, but
not hospitable and not popular. Their lives, indeed,
had been darkened by a great misfortune. They had
been married for many years before Elizabeth's birth,
and their first born child, and for a long time their
only child, had been a son. On this boy all their
hopes had centred,—and he had gone to utter ruin.
The story was never clearly told to any one, and
hardly any even of those who had been most intimate
with the Rivieres, knew the circumstances of the case

. . .

in any detail; they only knew that there had been some great tragedy; that young Riviere had been found one morning in his lodgings in London, lying dead; and that his father and mother from that time had given up the world, and all interest in it, and had buried themselves with their little girl in the quiet of their lonely country house.

So Elizabeth grew up there, with nothing but grave faces round her—her father and mother loving her with what heart they had left to love anything, but not showing that affection by much outward tenderness—and with no playmates or companions. It was a dull life,—only she had never been used to any other, and did not know that it was dull. The house and the grounds were large, and in summer she roamed about them, and in winter she curled herself into warm corners by the fire, and both winter and summer—in sunshine or by firelight—she dreamed dreams, such as girls who are left to their own fancies do dream, wonderful dreams of a world outside these walls, which she should see some day, and of joys and sorrows that should befall her in that vague future which she was always looking forward to, and which was always drawing nearer to her.

She was a girl of sixteen when for the first time something came and touched her life from that outer world.

"Your Uncle Garnett's son is coming to see us,

Elizabeth," her mother said suddenly to her one day. "We have not asked for the visit, but it has been offered to us, so we cannot refuse it. Your cousin is at Addiscombe, and his father wants him to spend his holidays here."

"I wonder if I shall like him!" was Elizabeth's thought.

He was to come in a fortnight, and during that fortnight she thought a great deal about this cousin. She wondered what he would do all the time he remained with them; she wondered if he and she would be much together, if he would talk much to her, if he would care for her at all. She was not used to companions, and when at the fortnight's end the handsome bright boy came, the first few days passed uneasily over their heads. The lad of eighteen was bored; the girl of sixteen was cold and shy. But she had a pair of eloquent dark eyes that presently, before her lips found many words to say, fell to speaking to him in their own language, and that language was one that Harry Garnett—full of vanity and the love of admiration, as well as of better things—soon began to find it very pleasant to interpret. "You are so clever and good and beautiful," they said; "you have seen so much; you know so many things. Ah, you are so much better than I am! I feel beside you as if I could do nothing, and as if you—you could do everything." This was how they unconsciously talked

to him all day. The boy began to understand them
very quickly, and then what was natural quickly followed: his vanity was touched first, and something
next that was better than his vanity. She was little
more than a child, yet heaven opened to her during
these summer days. When at the end of his holidays
the young cadet went back to Addiscombe, he took
Elizabeth's young heart with him, and the half of a
broken sixpence.

He was a clever, quick, light-hearted boy, very
bright and very loveable. Such a lad becoming intimate with a girl brought up like Elizabeth Riviere,
was almost certain to make her care for him: that she
should make *him* care for *her*, or that, having gained
his love once, she should succeed—young and volatile
as he was—in retaining it, was, at the beginning, less
probable; yet, to his honour, he remained true to her.
For two years he continued to come, whenever it was
possible for him to do so, to the Rivieres', and then,
at the end of that time, when his career at Addiscombe was ended, and he was about to sail for India,
the young man on his last visit went boldly to Mr.
Riviere, and asked him for his daughter's hand.

The two young people had agreed together that
this was the proper and honourable course to pursue,
so Harry Garnett, feeling rather more nervous than
he would have confessed, solicited an interview one
morning with his uncle, and having been brought face

to face with him, made the request that both to himself and Elizabeth beforehand had seemed so sensible,
that no reasonable person could refuse it.
Mr. Riviere, perhaps, however, was *not* reasonable.
At any rate his only answer to the young man's
speech, was the quiet and rather contemptuous question:

"And what are the means, may I take the liberty
of asking, upon which you propose to support my
daughter as your wife?"

The blood, at this enquiry, came up into young
Garnett's cheek. He and Elizabeth had settled this
question of means quite comfortably with one another
long ago. Elizabeth would be sure to have enough
given to her by her father to live upon, and Harry
would have his lieutenant's pay, which would become
captain's and major's and colonel's pay, of course, in
time. The matter had seemed, whenever they had
talked it over, perfectly plain and simple; yet somehow now, when Mr. Riviere sat opposite to him, and
put his cold and sarcastic question, young Garnett felt
it less easy than he had expected it would be to ex-
plain to him the little plan that Elizabeth and he had
laid. Instead of explaining it at all, indeed, he only
turned red, and after some moments of hesitation,
blurted out—

"Of course you know, sir, what I have at present——"

"I should have thought I did," Mr. Riviere courteously replied. "Only as you propose to marry Elizabeth, I must presume that you possess some source of
income which is unknown to me."

"Sir, you are trying to turn me into ridicule!"
the young man interrupted him hotly.

"Your request is ridiculous enough, without my
needing to throw any fresh ridicule upon it," Mr.
Riviere answered with perfect equanimity. "Harry
Garnett, you are making a fool of yourself. Your
cousin Elizabeth, should she ever marry, will bring a
fortune to her husband of thirty thousand pounds.
When *you* possess thirty thousand pounds you may
come to me again, and ask me for her hand, and I
will treat your request then with gravity, at any rate;
but till that time comes you and my daughter shall
neither make love to one another, nor meet one another again. Now this is the whole of what I have to
say," and he rose up. "You needn't open your lips
to utter another word."

Young Garnett tried to plead his cause afresh, but
he tried in vain.

"Tut, tut, you and Elizabeth are a pair of children and a pair of fools," was all Mr. Riviere would
say; and when the young man would not hold his
peace, he took up his newspaper and left the room.

That afternoon Elizabeth and Harry Garnett
parted. The girl summoning all her courage before

he went away, went to her mother, and told her tale to her; but Mrs. Riviere took her husband's view of the matter, and, though she was not unkind to her daughter, called her a foolish child, and treated her poor little love story as a piece of utter folly. From her no hope nor comfort was to be got: so then there was nothing for the two young creatures to do, but to bid one another good-bye, with tears and anguish, and vows of mutual constancy. And then Harry Garnett sailed for India, and Elizabeth pined for a little while, and presently—the strong young heart reviving—settled down to patient hope and waiting.

And so years passed on, and her lover became to the girl, absent from her though he was, something about which every hope and every thought she had clustered—the centre light of her life. His image as she grew older did not become more faint, but rather stood out in ever higher and stronger relief: to her imagination he became year by year more of a hero. Her fancy was for ever exalting him, her love for ever paying homage to him, and picturing him as greater and better and wiser than he was.

When I first saw Elizabeth, Harry Garnett had been in India for six years. She was a woman then of four-and-twenty, a handsome, accomplished, bright-witted woman. I had heard her story before I knew her, and I remember feeling some surprise the day we first met to find how free her whole expression

and manners were from anything like weariness or
dejection. She did not look like a girl who had been
separated from her lover for half a dozen years. She
was so full of light and energy, with large sweet intel-
lectual eyes that had a frank healthiness in them pleasant to look at.

It was at a dinner party in London, at the house
of a friend where she was staying, that I saw her. I
had entered the room a little late, and we had had no
conversation together before dinner, but when we had
left the table and had returned upstairs, she of her
own accord came and sat down beside me. She had
heard of me often, she said, and had wanted to know
me; and then we began to talk together, and I liked
the girl. I had been predisposed in her favour before
we met,—for I too had heard of her years before this
time,—yet I had scarcely expected to find her all that
I did, so large brained as well as large hearted, so
honest, frank, and simple.

The acquaintance that was begun that night between us, ripened soon after into intimacy. Her home
was still in the north, and she was not often in London, yet in the course of the next two years she came
to stay with me more than once, and during these
visits she often talked to me of Harry Garnett. He had
kept up the habit, throughout the whole time of his
absence, of writing occasionally to Mr. Riviere, and
by means of these letters she had always been able at

intervals to hear of him. The girl knew by heart all the main events of his life since he went away, and would often sit and talk of them to me with an intensity of interest that many a day brought the light to her eyes and the colour to her cheek. To myself, I confess, the deeds of the young hero became at times a little wearisome, related to me as they were, with a minuteness of detail and a lavishness of comment that only a love for him as great as Elizabeth's own could relish; but if I got tired of the often repeated stories now and then, I never let her know that: it made her so unspeakably happy to talk of her lover, that I never had the heart to rob her of a grain of her content.

She loved him with a healthy, brave, strong; patient love that was beautiful to witness, and that was as free from mere sentimentalism as any love I ever knew. She believed in him, long unseen as he was, as if she had only parted from him yesterday. I remember I asked her one day—feeling in myself a certain amount of doubt about the matter—whether she was quite sure that she should even know him again, if they were to meet now, and as I spoke she laughed, with such a happy unhesitating laugh as almost made me ashamed of my own suspicions.

"Do you suppose I expect to see him look the same now that he did at twenty?" she said. "Of course he will be altered. But as for not knowing

16*

him—" And then the quick bright colour leapt up to her face.

I said no more, but still the thought often returned to me, and I used to wonder many a time, if, when Harry Garnett came home, he would indeed prove in all respects the knight of Elizabeth Riviere's dreams, as wise and brave and good as she pictured him in her glowing thoughts.

He was Captain Garnett at this time, but, as far as I could learn, or as Elizabeth knew, he was very far indeed yet from being in a position to claim her hand. If she had been less sanguine than she was by nature, the knowledge of this would have weighed heavily upon her, but, except at rare moments, I always found her singularly hopeful. "I think if he were to come home in a few more years, when he is a little better off, papa would let me marry him," she said to me very simply once. "I don't believe that papa ever literally meant that he must have as much as I have before he would let me be married; I think he only meant that Harry must have—a little more, you know, than he had when he wanted me to be his wife first."

"He certainly had not much at that time," I replied drily, and then she laughed.

"Ah, I daresay it was very foolish, but we were both so young then," she said.

Her perfect trust in him, and her confidence in

his continued love for her were beautiful to see. She never doubted him for one moment. Before they parted, they had arranged that his letters to her father should be a sign that he remained true to her: until they ceased, she was to believe in him, he said, and they had never ceased. There was something touching in the pride with which the girl dwelt on this. Her lover was to her a miracle of constancy. "Think of all the other girls he must have seen, of the gay busy life he must lead, and yet of his remaining true to *me*," she would say. Her own truth she never thought anything of; that seemed to her only a perfectly natural thing.

The story of these two young people was one that interested me, and I often longed to reach the end of it, and to see my favourite made happy. Two years had passed since I had become acquainted with her, and as yet the matter—as far as any one could see—was no nearer than ever to its termination. While we were wholly unsuspicious of it, however, the denouement was in reality close at hand.

Elizabeth was staying with me in the summer that completed the eighth year of their separation, when one afternoon, as we were sitting alone, a servant came into the room with a little note in her hand, and delivered it to Elizabeth, saying that a gentleman had given it to her who was waiting below.

For a moment as she received it, Elizabeth looked

at the writing outside the letter, and then I saw the
colour leaving her face. She started up from her seat
almost with a cry. "It is from Harry!" she said, with
a wild look into my face.

I was not quite so agitated as she was, but I confess I was a good deal excited too at this sudden announcement. "From Harry Garnett! God bless me!"
I exclaimed; and then by that time Elizabeth had got
the letter opened.

It was a brief little pencilled note: I saw it afterwards.

"Elizabeth, will you come down and speak to
me?" it said. "I have just come from your father's,
where I went to find you. I landed from India three
days ago."

She was standing up, trembling all over.

"My dear, sit down again. Just stay quietly where
you are. I'll send him up to you," I said. And I
only stopped for one second to take her in my arms
and kiss her. As I ran downstairs I think I was for
the moment almost more happy than she was. I told
the servant to show Captain Garnett up to the drawing room, and then I stood and listened to his footsteps as he went up, and felt my heart beating almost
as if I had been Elizabeth herself when I heard the
door close behind him.

I went into the dining room, and sat down there
and sewed. I think I was very happy, but I was cer-

tainly at the same time very nervous. I longed to be
assured that all was right.' The time seemed very
long as I sat alone, waiting and wondering. Twice
had the clock struck before I at last heard Elizabeth's
step upon the stairs.

She guessed where I was, and came straight into
the room, my beautiful Elizabeth, not pale any more
now, but flushed like a red rose. She came in quickly,
and hurried up to me as if she did not want me to
look at her, and hid her face upon my neck.

"My darling," I said, "is it all right?"

"Oh yes, oh yes," she answered. And then she
gave something like a little gasp, and said, "His uncle
is dead and has left him almost rich, and so papa
says—" And then she fell to kissing me, a little hys-
terically, I thought.

"My dear," I cried, "I am almost as happy as you
are!"

I had scarcely thought she would have been so
much upset. For a few moments, before I saw her
face again, I think she was actually crying; she was
certainly still all trembling and nervous when she began to speak again.

"Will you come upstairs and see him?" she said.
"It was so good of you to leave us so long alone,
but—but I think we have had most of our talk out
now."

I rose up, and said that I should be delighted to see Captain Garnett,—though I smiled to myself at the simple little speech, as if a couple of hours were likely to exhaust their talk together!—and we went upstairs, and into the drawing room, and Mr. Garnett and I shook hands.

We shook hands very cordially, and I said something about the great pleasure that I had in seeing him; but I hardly know what there was in this first sight of him that should have surprised me so much as it certainly did. It was probably only that I had formed a wrong idea of him from Elizabeth's descriptions. I had never, indeed, taken those descriptions of hers quite *au pied de la lettre*, but still, making all due allowance for her enthusiasm, I confess I was for a moment taken aback by the very commonplace aspect of the handsome young man before me. That he *was* handsome, was unquestionable; but, to tell the truth, his beauty affected me much like the beauty of the blocks in a hair-dresser's shop. He was so oiled and curled, so white and pink, so perfect in costume and gallant in manner. I felt, after I had made him my little speech of welcome, as he stood bowing over my hand, smirking and smiling and showing his teeth, that I really did not know what to say next to him. "Well, every woman has her own notion of a hero," I thought to myself, as I made my way presently to a seat; but, with a vexed feeling of disappointment, I confessed to myself that certainly at this first sight of him, Harry Garnett was not mine.

We were going to dinner, and of course I asked Captain Garnett to stay, and he accepted the invitation with great alacrity, and not only stayed, but I must acknowledge, did his very best to make himself agreeable. During the whole of the evening, he was unremitting in his attentions, not only to Elizabeth but to me. I scarcely know to which of us he was the most tender, or made the greater number of pretty speeches. A more complete ladies' man I think I never saw. I protest, before he had been two hours in my company, he was winding silk for me, and counting the stitches for my Berlin work.

As for Elizabeth she was very quiet, more so than was usual with her, and not quiet only, but to some extent also unquestionably shy and nervous. It was very natural, perhaps, but yet it disturbed me a little too. When the tea tray was removed, I left the young people by themselves again for a time, thinking that that was probably the kindest thing I could do, and that Elizabeth would recover herself more quickly alone with her lover, than in the presence of any third person whatever; but I had not been downstairs for half an hour when the girl came in search of me, and begged me to return. "My dear child," I said to her, "you are far better without me." But she protested that it was not so; and it ended in my going

back with her to the drawing room, where we found
Captain Garnett beguiling the moments of our absence
with a novel. He was at home in all the light litera-
ture of the day, and indeed had a surface knowledge
of most things, and a power that I have never seen sur-
passed of talking glibly upon any subject under heaven.
He stayed with us till after ten o'clock, and then,
with what seemed to me a rather too profuse expression of the happiness he had enjoyed, he took his
leave of us. I could do no less, of course, than ask
him to return upon the following day, and this, with
a delighted smile, he instantly promised to do. He
was evidently ready to devote his whole time to Elizabeth, and to prove himself a most assiduous lover, so
assiduous that for a moment I thought inwardly with
some dismay, "I shall never have the house free from
him!" I must do myself the justice to say, however,
that I was angry at this thought as soon as I had
given expression to it; and to show my penitence before he went away, I pressed him—and I trust I did
it cordially—to spend as much of his time with us as
he felt inclined. "If it makes Elizabeth happy I am
sure I shall not mind it," I thought with some hero-
ism, resolved to face the prospect of Harry Garnett's
perpetual presence in my drawing room as bravely as
I could.

But *would* it make Elizabeth happy? She looked
agitated rather than happy when she and I were left

alone together. I was thinking to myself with a good deal of perplexity, "What am I to say to her?" I can't tell her the plain truth. What can I possibly say?" when she relieved me, for the moment at any rate, from my difficulty. Almost as soon as the door had closed upon her lover, she came to me, and with rather a tremulous smile, took my hand and said, "And now you must let me go straight to bed, for I am so bewildered that I feel as if my head was going round, and I hardly know whether I am awake or asleep. So kiss me, and say good night to me, and I'll go away."

I kissed her heartily, not sorry, certainly, to find her anxious to be alone; and with the tears in her eyes—for I said a few words to her such as I could say with truth from my very soul, and she was easily touched with kindness—she went up to her own room, and I sat after she was gone for half an hour alone, trying—but trying, I am afraid, for the most part, in vain—to swallow the feeling of disappointment that oppressed me. I could not do it. Reason as I would on the injustice of forming hasty judgments, I could not bring myself to believe that this superficial, shallow, commonplace young man, was a lover worthy of my deep-hearted Elizabeth. If *she* were satisfied with him, and saw in him the realization of her youthful dreams, of course I could have no word to say; all things considered, I could only be

thankful and rejoice; but then the question came
again, and I went to bed at last pondering and re-
volving it—*was* she satisfied?

Captain Garnett came to us next day at two o'clock.
I had expected him to make his appearance sooner,
but I suppose he was too correct a fine gentleman to
make a call upon the woman he was engaged to
marry, at an earlier hour than that. At any rate it
was two o'clock before we heard his dainty knock at
the door. He had a peculiarly dainty way of knock-
ing, as of doing all things. I always thought, when
on this and other days, I noticed him, that the action
of his white fingers was more like the action of the
fingers of a woman than a man. He was so curiously
neat and dexterous in every thing. Let him do what
he might, too, the thing was done prettily, from the
winding of silks to the carving of chickens, from the
mending of pens to the striking of guitar strings, he
did all so neatly and gracefully that it was a privilege
to see him. "I think you are one of the completest
creatures I ever knew!" I said to him one day in an
ecstasy of (perhaps, peculiar) admiration, when we had
become a good deal more intimate than we were yet;
and the young man laughed, and threw me a grateful
glance out of his tender blue eyes. I think he really
liked the compliment, and felt that I appreciated him
in paying it. And, in fact, I did appreciate him, and
feel to this day a certain genuine amount of admiration

for him, not by any means unmixed with liking. For
he *was* likeable. He had something lovable about him
in spite of his fopperies and his gallantry, and all his
other little shallow follies. He was not the hero that
Elizabeth Riviere thought him, but he was a sunny-
tempered, pleasan-tnatured creature, with enough
general cleverness to enable him to pick up an acquaintance with all sorts of things much in the rapid
way that a chicken picks up grains of corn, and with
a certain dexterity and tact that, like instinct, taught
him how to turn these many odds and ends of knowledge to account. Before I had known him four and
twenty hours I did not wonder that Elizabeth at
seventeen had made a hero of him: but what would
Elizabeth do now when she was six and twenty?

I watched her day after day, and I could not tell.
The girl, who had been full of frankness and unre-
serve to me before her lover came, had become suddenly like a sealed book. From that afternoon when
Harry Garnett first appeared, she never spoke his
name to me except as she might have spoken the
name of any other common friend we had; she never
sat at my feet to talk of his perfections, as she had
done a hundred times before; she never once asked
me what I thought of him. I could not tell with any
certainty what she was feeling. She did quietly all
she had to do, but she did it without any appearance
of joy. She was always very gentle to Captain Gar-

nett, but that very gentleness was a sign I did not like. She was too meek by half, too patient by nine-tenths. If I had seen her begin to tease or cross or worry him, I should have felt quite comfortable about her; but she never teased him, and he had his own way a hundred times oftener than was at all whole-some for him. If he expressed a desire, she acceded to it; if he asked her to do this or that she did it; if he even gave vent to opinions (and he did so fre-quently) with which she did not agree, she rarely dis-puted them with him. And yet I could not tell if she was unhappy. After a fashion she seemed to me to love the man, though it was after a fashion all unlike what I should have expected from her. Her gentleness to him was often mixed with tenderness, though the tenderness was always, it seemed to me, half sad. I saw her put her hand upon his brow one day, and look into his eyes, and heard her say to him, "Harry, you have kept yourself so young!" in a tone that seemed to me to have a curious regretful pathos in it. But, if it was so, *his* ears at least did not catch it. "Have I?" he only replied, and laughed contentedly. He thought she was saying something kind to him.

I wondered for a time whether her manner to him satisfied young Garnett. He was himself extremely *empressé* in his demeanour to her, tender to a pro-voking extent, I always thought, and as inseparable from her when he was in the house as her shadow;

but after a few days had passed, it often seemed to me (unless I was labouring under a delusion altogether) that he was trying her almost to the last point of endurance. His loverlike dallyings, his holdings of her hand, his whispers in her ear, seemed to become at moments more than she could bear. And, to tell the truth, I felt sometimes that if I had been in Elizabeth's place, I should have boxed his ears. To have him hanging over me, doing nothing himself, and meddling with all that *I* was doing, disturbing my workbasket, or throwing my pens and paper into confusion, and smiling in my face all the while, and uttering his little flighty foolish gallantries, would, though I really liked the creature, have almost made me stick needles into him. Elizabeth was affected by his ways, perhaps, a little differently, but yet even she —or else I was very far wrong—found them hard to bear. And in truth she sometimes did not bear them. During the second week that he was coming about her, I more than once saw her get up from his side and leave the room.

I was sorely puzzled what to do. Every day made my heart heavier for my poor girl; but yet she was no child now to whom I could have given counsel, but a grown woman, as capable of managing her own affairs as any woman I ever knew. The more I saw her with Captain Garnett, the more I feared that the sight of him had destroyed the dream she had che-

rished so long; but how could she break off an eight
years' engagement, and jilt a man who had been so
long faithful to her?

I suppose this was the question that she was
ceaselessly asking herself through these restless and
unhappy days. Once or twice I tried to approach the
subject with her, but she would not allow me to do
it. In all probability she suspected my design, and
so was on her guard. She gave me no opportunity
whatever of penetrating into her confidence.

The matter had gone on for three weeks when at
length an evening came that seemed to try Elizabeth's
powers of endurance more (and this is saying a good
deal) than even any previous one had done. She was
not well that night, I think; she was tired with the
day's occupation—we had all been out somewhere
together; the night was sultry, and she was irritable
and worn out.

All this Captain Garnett ought to have understood,
but he did not. He perceived, indeed, poor fellow,
that she was tired and cross, but his perception of
this only had the effect of making him more than
usually intolerable in his attentions to her, for, instead
of leaving her alone, which was the only thing she
wanted, he literally buzzed about her like a fly. She
could not move her finger but he flew to her; if she
rose from her seat, he sprang up too; when she lay
down on the sofa, as she did after tea (thinking, per-

haps, poor soul, that she should get rid of him that way) he hung over her, and fidgeted with her pillows, and kissed her hands, and whispered in her ear till I think she was half wild.

Amongst intolerable things, I fancy few can be more intolerable than to be forced to sit still and let a man you do not love make love to you. Elizabeth had submitted to this penance for three weeks; I, in her place, I think, would not have borne it for three days, at least I would not have borne it from Captain Garnett; for there was something to me about his love-making that was irritating beyond all expression, it had such a character of boyishness about it; it was so persistent, so silly, so sentimental. The man in other ways was not by any means a fool, but devotion and tenderness, he always seemed to think, were only to be shown by divesting himself of everything like manliness or common sense.

I never was so thankful for the ending of any evening since Captain Garnett's advent as I was, when it came, for the ending of this one.

"Elizabeth is very tired to-night, and I am going to send you away early," I said to him when it drew towards ten o'clock, and with some difficulty—for, in spite of the small response she made to him, he showed himself more than usually unwilling to depart —I got him out of the house.

During the last half hour of his stay Elizabeth
had scarcely spoken to him. She was sitting by an
open window (for she had risen restlessly from the
sofa some time before) with her face turned from the
room, and gradually she had grown so silent that at
last he had had to content himself mainly with talking to me instead of her, although every few minutes,
with an unfortunate aptitude for doing a wrong thing,
he continued to find some new way of worrying and
fretting her. Again and again I saw him try in the
twilight to take her hand, and again and again I
noticed her, on some pretext or other, draw it away
from him. She was certainly in no humour that hot
June night to sit hand in hand with Harry Garnett.

However, it came to an end at last. As the clock
was striking ten I got him on his feet. "We shall be
quit of him now in another minute," I thought to
myself; but before that minute had passed Elizabeth
had said something that on a sudden made my heart
beat quick.

He had begun to murmur some last tender no-
things over her, when in the midst of them, as if she
was scarcely conscious that he was speaking (as very
likely, I think, she was not), she interrupted him.
There was only a faint light in the room, coming
from a single lamp at some distance from her—for
the June twilight had scarcely passed away yet—so
that I could not see her face distinctly, but yet it

seemed to me, in the sudden sight that I had of it as she turned round, startlingly hard and white.

She said abruptly—

"I want to say something to you. Will you come early to-morrow. Will you come here at ten o'clock?"

She had struck into the midst of his little tender cooings without being in the least aware of it. Possibly for a moment he might have been hurt, but if he was he recovered himself immediately.

"At ten o'clock?" he repeated. "Oh yes, certainly, if you wish it."

"Then come," she said. "And good night now." And then she took his hand, and urged by something —some sudden feeling of remorse perhaps—held it for two or three moments very closely.

Poor lad!—he went away unsuspicious and happy. As the door closed behind him Elizabeth's face was covered by her hands, and I heard one great stifled sob; but I moved about the room for a few moments, setting this and that thing in order, and by the time a minute had gone past she had regained her self possession and had risen up.

She came to me and said merely—"Will you let me go to bed now, for I am so very tired?"

She indeed looked tired; it made my heart ache to see her.

"Yes—go to bed, my darling," I replied; and then

17*

I took her in my arms, and I think I was nearer crying than she was when she went away from me.

Well—on that next morning she broke off her engagement. Until it was done she and I spoke no word together about it: she wanted no advice nor assistance from me, and I offered her none. But when all was over she told me what had passed during that last hard and sad interview between herself and Captain Garnett.

He came true to his time. We had had breakfast together before his arrival, but she had scarcely opened her lips either to eat or speak. She looked so ill too that I was uneasy about her, and began to fear that she might not have strength to go through the task that she had set herself. Nothing that I or any one could do, however, could help her, so I held my tongue; and at ten o'clock Harry Garnett came. We were sitting in the dining room, but I had given orders that when he arrived he should be taken upstairs. As she heard his knock I saw Elizabeth's face flush scarlet, and I longed to go to her and try to comfort her, but I did not dare lest I should make her break down. I only took her hand for one moment and pressed it in mine, as, when she had risen up, she passed my chair.

She left me and went straight upstairs, and into the room where Captain Garnett was waiting. Then what followed was something like this:

He came forward to meet her with his usual smile, but changed his expression suddenly when he reached her, startled by the strange look upon her face.

"My darling," he said hurriedly, "is anything wrong?"

That question "Is anything wrong" must have struck terribly to her heart at once. Poor soul, every thing was wrong, and she had to tell him so, and, blameless as he was, to wound him to the quick. It was hard to do—harder, very likely, when the actual moment had come at last than she had even pictured it beforehand as being. But it was no use to hesitate then.

She began almost at once to speak to him.

"Harry," she said, "I asked you to come here this morning because—because I have done you a great wrong, and I want to tell you of it before it gets made worse even than it is now. I have made a terrible mistake, and I want to undo it. Harry," she said almost below her breath, "I shall startle you at first,—but you must let it be as I say: I want to break our engagement off."

"You want to do *what?*" he exclaimed.

He had sat down beside her, but as he spoke he started to his feet.

"Break off our engagement! Good heavens, Elizabeth, are you mad?" he said.

"No, I am not mad," she answered sadly. "I am

only half broken-hearted. Do you think I would say this to you if I could help it—if I saw any thing else that it was possible for me to do? Oh Harry," she cried suddenly. "I have suffered so! All this time that you have been coming here, day after day, have you never seen that I was unhappy?—have you never seen that I have not cared for you as you have cared for me?"

He was standing looking at her blankly, all bewildered,—her great fault, his own ill treatment, as yet almost unrealized. For in spite of her not unfrequent coldness to him he had never until now, I think, had a moment's real doubt of her affection: it never, I am sure, had occurred to him as a possibility that she should wish to throw him off. Perhaps it had been in a large measure his vanity that had made him trust her so implicitly; but yet there was, too, a sort of instinctive trustfulness of nature about him that always—though it was half childish—seemed to me a lovable kind of thing.

"You have not cared for me!" he began to exclaim. "Not cared for me! Why,—if there was one thing more than another that I thought you wanted me to believe—if there was one thing that I thought was certain—it was that all these eight years—"

"That I loved you all these eight years?" she interrupted him sadly. "Ah, yes,—that *is* certain: I have told you that;—and I would tell it you again now, if you like,—and a thousand times again! Oh

Harry, I have not deceived you there. I loved what
I *thought* you—as passionately as ever any woman
did. You had been the idol of my girlhood, and
through all these years—through every day of these
years —you have been the light of my life—till now."

She said these last words slowly, and when she
had said them she hid her face suddenly upon her
hands, and burst into a great passion of tears,—weeping, I think, for herself rather than for him,—in self-
pity for the loss of that dream of her life which at
this moment seemed to her to be the loss of everything that made the world dear.

He sat down beside her again, and tried to soothe
her. He could not understand her yet,—she mystified
him utterly,—he did not know what she meant; but
at least the sight of her distress moved him. He
would have taken her in his arms and caressed her, if
she would have let him. When she would not he still
sat by her side, but a dark look for the first time
began to come on his face.

"Harry, cannot you understand me?" she said beseechingly to him presently. "Cannot you see how it
has all been? I have been wrong—oh, I know I have
been wrong!" she cried bitterly; "but I was so young
when you went away. How could I judge of you
when I was such a child? I thought I could,—and I
have foolishly gone on thinking so all these years,—
but I know that I could not now. Harry, can you

not understand me, and forgive me? I meant so to
be true to you. God knows if I ever meant anything
in this world I meant that. And I *have* been true to
my idea of you;—only it has been a wrong idea."

"And so you think yourself justified in throwing
me off!" he said indignantly.

"Justified!" she repeated slowly. "No—I may not
be justified,—but what else can I do? You think I
am wronging you,—and I *am* wronging you; but in
doing it do *I* not suffer more bitterly than *you?*
What are you losing compared with what *I* have lost?
You were all the world to me—the one love of my
life. And now what have I to hope for? It is as if
the light had gone out that had been to me as the
sun in heaven!"

This was the gist of what she said to him. They
talked for a long while, but all the rest was but a
repetition of this. He on his part argued and en-
treated, and finally, as she had expected, rose to leave
her in a passion of anger. He could not forgive her,
or feel any sympathy for her.

"You have used me scandalously," he said to her.
"You have kept me bound to you for eight years,
and now you throw me off as I think—thank God!—
not another woman in five hundred would! You have
no justification for what you are doing. I give you
leave, if you like, to tell the story to fifty people, and
see if one of them would side with you!"

Before he spoke like this, I do him the justice to say, he had done his utmost to change her resolution, and had even for a time been patient and tender with her,—for the man had honestly, after his fashion, loved my poor Elizabeth, and her rejection of him wounded more than his vanity. He had urged her not to break with him with all the eloquence he possessed. But when, though she wept as he talked, she would not let his eloquence move her, then at last he became indignant. He was going to leave the room when he had uttered these words that I have repeated, and he would have left it, if she had allowed him; but she loved him still too well to let him go from her like that. She went up to him entreatingly, holding out both her hands.

"Harry, you must not go away with these for your last words," she said to him. "If I will not marry you (and I only will not because I dare not), you are still more to me than all the rest of the world. I never can be indifferent to you—I never can forget you. Will you not believe me? When the soreness of all this has passed, and—and some one else has made you happier than I could ever make you, will you not forgive me, Harry, and let us be friends again?"

She clung to him as she spoke: she seemed to forget that they were about to part, and that all was ended between them: in her earnestness she held his hand clasped closely in both of hers.

For a few moments he made no answer. He probably did not want to be harsh to her, but yet he could not forgive her: as was natural enough he even exaggerated to himself the wrong that she had done him.

"You have taken all the hope out of my life," he said to her. "You are the only woman that I care for, and you are treating me as badly as if you were the most heartless flirt alive. Elizabeth, I have not deserved this from you. I have been true to *you*, whatever my shortcomings or my faults may be."

"Yes—you have been true to me: do you suppose the thought of that does not wring my heart?" she said. "You have been always true to me—always good to me—and I seem to be returning nothing to you but falsehood and evil. Oh Harry, that is the bitterest part of it all! I want to do right; yet I cannot even do right now without doing first what seems a great wrong."

They stood in silence after this for a few moments longer, and then she clasped his hand again, and said to him—

"Let us say good bye to one another now."

She was so humble that she put his hand to her lips and kissed it before she let it go. She said to him, with her voice trembling, "God bless you for ever and ever."

I asked her whether he spoke any last words of kindness or forgiveness before he left her, but she burst into tears, and answered "No."

This was the end of Elizabeth Riviere's love story. Her engagement had been known to many people, and when her breaking of it became known too, her conduct was widely criticized, and widely condemned. I have always found that even where her story has been told fairly the greater number of those who hear it refuse their sympathy to her. "She undoubtedly treated the man badly," they say. "The mistake that she made was an inexcusable mistake." Grant, however, that the mistake *was* inexcusable, still in what she did was she not more right than wrong? She had placed herself (by her own fault, if you like,) in a position from which no move she might have made —let her act as she would—could have been wholly right. But I thought from the first, and I think still, that she did a better, and I am sure she did a braver, thing in breaking with Harry Garnett, as she did, at all costs, than if she had married him with nothing remaining in her heart of her old love.

Captain Garnett did not continue long inconsolable after her rejection of him. He married within a year after Elizabeth and he had parted, and I hear that he and his wife are a pair of very happy people. As for Elizabeth she has reached the age of thirty-four, and she is Elizabeth Riviere still.   I do not think that she will ever marry now.   In giving her lover up, and in losing what had for so long made the light and glory of her life, she suffered a hundred times more than he did: but that, of course, was only just, and I ask no one who is disinclined to do so either to pity her for her loss, or to forgive her fault.

END OF "WAS ELIZABETH RIGHT?"

LITTLE BARBARA.

LITTLE BARBARA.

Do you remember the pretty old nursery story of the Babes in the Wood? Well, there are other *new* stories of little lost children quite as pretty as that one, and true too. Here is one that I heard somewhere not long ago.

There were three young children who lived in a cottage in a very lonely place. It was so quiet a place that sometimes for days together they never saw any other faces except their own and their father's and mother's; especially in winter, when the snow lay deep upon the ground. Often, then, not a sound would be heard from morning to night, and not a footstep would pass their door.

The little house stood high upon a hillside, and in these lonely days the children would sometimes say to one another, "I wish we lived down in the village; it would be so much merrier there." And they would often go about a quarter of a mile from the cottage, where they could see a good way down the hill, and would stand there watching the little specks of people below, and wondering what every one was doing, and thinking that it must be very pleasant, when the snow lay so deep that they could not play out in the wood, to have the nice village street to run about in, and to be able to look through the cottage windows at the bright fires blazing within. In the summer they never longed to go to the village, for then they had plenty of delights at home. They were very poor,—so poor that they often had not bread enough to eat, nor clothes enough to keep them warm, but yet in the summer they were always happy. It did not matter to them, then, that their little frocks were thin, and their little shoes worn; it hardly seemed to matter even that their porridge came so soon to an end, and that the potatoes at dinner seemed never to be enough for all of them; for were there not always wild fruits in the wood, and thousands of red and purple berries good to eat? They used to eat them by the hour together; and by the hour together, too, they would gather the beautiful wild wood-flowers and play with them, and make chains and garlands of them, sitting on the grass or on the moss at the roots of the great trees. They would often spend the whole of long summer days like this, never wandering so far away from home but that their mother's voice could reach them if she stood at the outskirts of the wood and called, but yet often out of sight for hours together, hidden by the thick branches, or sometimes almost buried amidst the brushwood and the long green grass.

"Some day I should like to walk straight forward, whole miles into the forest," the eldest of the children would say sometimes to her mother; but the mother would always very cautiously shake her head. "*I* have lived here for ten years, my dear," she would answer, "and I have never once been for miles into the forest."

They were two girls and a boy. The eldest girl, Barbara, was four years older than the others; she was almost nine. The other girl came next,—a little thing of five, called Lizzy; and then came the boy, David, who was scarcely four. The two young ones were always given into Barbara's charge when they went for their long play-days into the wood, and a very tender, careful nurse she was to them. She was a sweet-tempered, thoughtful, sensible little thing, with a grave, pretty face, and curious womanly ways, such as the children of poor people often get when they are very young. She was so used to having her mother depend upon her, and trust in her watchfulness and good sense, that I think for nearly a couple of years back she had almost forgotten that she was a child, and had got to have quite the staid manners of a grown-up person. "I don't know what I should do without Barbara," the mother would often gratefully say.

It had been summer, but the summer was almost gone, and the leaves were all yellow in the wood, and the days were getting cold. The children liked the early part of autumn dearly, for the fruits were ripest then, and the flowers brightest; but when the days began to grow very short, and November winds blew, and dead leaves lay thick on the damp ground, then it was sometimes rather dreary in the forest, and they were often glad to come home, and play instead by their own fireside.

"It will soon be winter now in real earnest," the mother said, one evening when they had been forced to close the cottage door because the wind blew in so coldly; and she sighed as she said it, for the winter often brought them hard times, and both she and the children would have had it summer always if they could.

It had been a raw wintry day. For several hours rain had been falling, and then after the rain there came a sudden frost, that made all the ground almost as slippery as glass. They sat waiting in the firelight for the father to come home. They looked for him always soon after nightfall, but to-night it had been quite dark for more than an hour, and yet he had not come. Again and again the mother went to the door to listen for him, but there was no sound of any step coming near. It was almost eight o'clock before he came at last, limping painfully up the steep path.

"I've fallen down and hurt my knee. I thought I should never get home," he called out to his wife as soon as he got near.

He was quite white and faint when he came into the cottage. "I slipped when I was two thirds up the hill," he said. "I've been trying to crawl on ever since. I don't know if I've broken a bone, or what it is,—but I'm glad to have got home at last."

His wife got him to bed, and bathed and bandaged the knee, and after a time he had less pain.

"I dare say I've only given it a twist," he said, presently, "and maybe it will be well by morning."

But when morning came the pain had come back, and the limb was swollen and useless. All that day he lay in bed, and by night-time he was very feverish. They had yet sent for no doctor, for, poor as they were, and living in such a solitary place, they rarely thought of sending for one when they were ill, but doctored themselves as they best could. But now the poor wife began to get frightened. Her husband tossed about on his bed all night, and the more restless he was, the more he suffered, for every movement that he made sharpened his pain.

She sat up with him all the night, and then in the morning at last she said to Barbara,—

"You must go down to the village, and ask Mr. Dickson to come and see him, for I'm sure he's getting worse."

So little Barbara put on her bonnet and cloak and prepared to go upon her errand.

It was a dull, cold morning,—very cold. The

frost had passed away now, but there were leaden clouds over the sky that seemed to promise snow, and the wind was very cutting and keen.

"You might take the children with you as far as to Mrs. Pope's," the mother said as Barbara was putting on her bonnet, "and call for them again as you come back. Tell Mrs. Pope about your father, and say I'd be obliged if she'd take care of them for an hour or two."

Then Barbara dressed the little ones too, and they set out.

"I'll be back, mother, as soon as ever I can," she said as she left the house.

It was about twelve o'clock of a November morning. The cottage at which Barbara was to leave the children was only about a mile away, standing, as their own did, close to the forest. It was a house to which they often went, for the people who lived in it —an old man and his wife—were their nearest neighbors, and very kind and good-natured ones. It was no uncommon thing, when the mother sent Barbara on any message to the village, for her to leave her little brother and sister here to rest while she went on by herself the two miles farther; and the whole little journey to the village and back—six miles in all—used to be made easily by her in about three hours. To-day, as she left home at twelve o'clock, she ought to be back, if she did not linger,—and on such a day she was sure not to linger,—soon after three. But when three o'clock arrived, she had not returned. About four o'clock the doctor came, and the mother, half uneasy by this time, said to him,—

"Did you not overtake my little girls coming home?"

No, he answered, he had seen nobody.

Then he examined her husband's knee, and told her what to do for it. As he was going away, he glanced up at the sky while she held the door open for him, and said, carelessly,—

"We shall have snow before night, I think."

"O, I wish my children were at home!" the mother cried, with a sudden fear.

"Where do you suppose they are? The little girl was with me hours ago," he said.

And then she told him that she supposed they must have been persuaded to stay at her neighbor's cottage,—though it was not like Barbara, she said, who was so thoughtful always.

"O, well, don't you frighten yourself," the doctor answered, good-naturedly. "I'll knock at Mrs. Pope's just now as I pass, and send them home to you."

And then he went away, and when he got to Mrs. Pope's he stopped at the door and knocked.

"You've got Mrs. Morris's children with you here, haven't you?" he said. "Tell them to run away home, for their mother wants them."

"*I* got the children, sir!" Mrs. Pope exclaimed. "I haven't seen them!"

"Why, she sent them here this morning," the doctor said.

"Then they never got in, sir, for I've been down in the village all the morning," she answered, "and had the house shut up, and the key in my pocket."

It was half past four o'clock, and the short November day was already ending. The doctor gave a quick look towards the forest.

"If they have lost themselves wandering about there, with the night coming on—" he said, suddenly.

But Mrs. Pope shook her head. "I don't think they can have lost themselves, sir," she answered. "Why, little Barbara is as steady as a woman; she'd no more go into a part of the wood where she didn't know her way than I would. I'll tell you what I dare say she's done. I think that she's taken the children with her down to the village, and they've been resting somewhere for a bit. I wish they were at home, for the night's coming on fast; but I don't believe they can be in the forest, sir."

The doctor was busy, and had no more time to waste.

"Well, if they've all been to the village together I may meet them yet," he said; "and if I do I'll hurry them home."

And then he bade Mrs. Pope good night, and

hastened on. But he did not meet the children on his way. Neither he nor any one else ever met the three little figures again, coming up the steep path.

It was half past twelve o'clock when Barbara reached Mrs. Pope's cottage. She knocked at the door, but no one, of course, opened it.

"O dear!" Barbara exclaimed, "she's not at home!" And, then, quite puzzled what to do, she stood with the two little ones at her side. She thought at first that she must take them home again; but then it would delay her so in fetching the doctor, for it was such a long way home. She could not take them to the village with her, for the only time that she had tried to do that Davie had broken down upon the road, and she had had to carry him in her arms till she could scarcely stand. Suppose she left them here outside the cottage to run about and play till Mrs. Pope should come back and take them in? She thought the question over in her grave little mind for two or three minutes, and then at last she resolved that she *would* leave them here. The poor child was so anxious to get the doctor for her father that at the moment that seemed to her more important than any other thing. Her father was so ill; if she could only get the doctor quickly!

"Lizzy," she said to her little sister, "if I leave you and Davie here to play till I come back, will you be sure to keep inside the garden, and not go anywhere out of sight?"

"O yes!" answered Lizzy, readily.

"I'll come back as fast as ever I can," poor Barbara promised; "and mind, I shall be so angry if you don't do what I tell you. Now you understand?"

"O yes!" said Lizzy again.

"And you're to take care of Davie, you know, and not let him stir a step beyond the gate or get into any mischief. I shall be back very soon; I sha'n't be more than an hour away," said the elder sister. And then, half uneasy, and yet not knowing what else she could do, she closed the little garden gate upon the children, and hurried away.

She ran half way to the doctor's house, and half way back again. She was tired and breathless when she got once more to Mrs. Pope's cottage. The garden door was standing open, and the children were not in the garden; but she said to herself, "O, Mrs. Pope has come back; that is all right," and went quickly up to the house door and knocked. But no one answered her knock. With the color leaving her face, she went round to the window and looked in. No one was there; the fire had not been touched; the house was empty.

She stood still for a minute, and in her sudden fear burst into tears. She was too startled at first to do anything else. But when that first minute had passed she began to get back her courage. "O, they shouldn't have gone away when I told them not!" she said to herself. "They must have gone into the wood, — and Lizzy promised me that she wouldn't," she said, reproachfully, as she ran back again to the garden gate to begin her search for them.

She was not very much frightened now, for she and her brother and sister had often before played in this part of the forest that was close to Mrs. Pope's house, and she thought that very likely the children had only gone a very little way in, and that she should find them before many minutes. So she went in amongst the trees, and began to call, "Lizzy! Lizzy!" and then "Davie! Davie! don't you hear me?" thinking every moment that their voices would come back to answer her.

But no answer came, though she went on calling till she was tired. Then she began to get frightened again, and went backwards and forwards searching for them everywhere, and began to pierce into parts of the forest where she had never been before, so eager to find them that she quite forgot that she was losing her own way, and that the trees were closing in all round her.

She had been looking for them for a long time,— or at least for what to her seemed a long time,— when at last she heard a little sound that she thought was Davie's voice. It was a faint sound of crying far away. She had been standing still listening, not knowing in her terror what to do next, wondering whether it would be best for her to go home and see if they might have got there before her, and yet feeling as if her heart would break if she should get .home and find they weren't there,—when this feeble little voice reached her, and made her heart leap to her lips with joy.

"O Davie! yes, I hear you!" she cried out, and then she ran to where the voice seemed to come from, and as she ran she heard it again and again, till at last she caught sight of the two little ones standing sobbing, with their arms stretched out to her.

"O Lizzy, how could you break your promise?" Barbara said, and burst out crying again as she caught little Davie up.

"It was a hare amongst the trees, sister," David said, as soon as he could speak. "I saw it, and I was tired of staying in the garden, and I ran after it, and Lizzy ran too,—and we lost our way."

"I couldn't help it. Davie would come; I couldn't stop him," Lizzy said, half sobbing.

Barbara did not scold the children; she was too glad to have found them again to do that. She stood holding their hands, one in each of hers, feeling for the moment quite happy again. They were all tired, and she was quite breathless, and for a few minutes she

leant against the trunk of one of the big trees to rest.
Then presently she said,—

"Mother will think we are never coming back. We
must get home now as fast as ever we can."

And still holding little Davie's hand, she took a
step or two forward, till all at once she thought with
a great start, "Which *is* the way home?" and then
stood suddenly still. Was it this way through the tall
fir-trees? or down there where there seemed to be a
kind of pathway through the brushwood? She did
not know. She looked up to the sky, but the sky
was covered with leaden clouds; there was no sun
there to guide her. "I think I will go through the
brushwood," she said to herself at last, with a great
fear beginning to come over her; and then she went
on, while the children followed her, and little Davie
chattered to her in his piping voice, beginning to forget his fright and sorrow.

For a few minutes they all walked on; then Lizzy
suddenly said, "I don't think this was the way we
came."

"Was it not?" Barbara asked, quickly, and, looking round with her anxious face, stood still again.

Till now she had not told her sister that she had
lost the way, but now, all at once, when she stood
still, Lizzy pressed up to her.

"Sister, don't you know how to go?" she said,
with great eyes lifted up to Barbara's face. And

then, when Barbara did not answer, the little one began
to cry.

"Hush, dear! it will all come right. I'll find the
way presently. I've only lost it for—·for a little while,"
poor Barbara said; and she took a hand of Lizzy too,
and went on again, trying to follow the feebly traced
pathway that was her only guide; but that was leading
her—she did not know where.

The cold and dreary November afternoon grew
colder and drearier still. All day there had been a
biting northeast wind, and it came whistling now
through the leafless branches, piercing through the
children's little coats till their teeth chattered, and
they shivered with cold.

"O, I want to get home!" Davie began to sob.
"I so tired, I want to get home!" And he stopped
at last, and threw his arms round Barbara's waist, and
leaned his weary little head against her side.

Then she took him up and carried him. He was
a heavy boy of four, and she was only nine, but she
patiently carried him, and hushed him on her bosom
as she went on. She had no longer even that faint
trace of a pathway to lead her now; it had ceased, or
she had lost it, and in all that great wilderness of
trees there was no sign left to guide them. She
wandered on, backwards and forwards, not knowing
any more how she went, the great sick fear in her
heart growing greater and bitterer with every step she

took. All the way she kept crying piteously to herself,—what was she to do, O what was she to do, if
she should never find the lost way home?

Little Lizzy kept moaning and sobbing at her side.
Davie fell presently half asleep in her tired arms.
Once or twice, almost exhausted, she sat down for a
little while upon the ground, but, weary as she was,
she did not dare to rest for more than a few moments.
How could she rest when the night was so near?
After each little pause she rose up hurriedly, and
toiled on again. Perhaps throughout these miserable
hours the hardest thought she had to bear was the
thought that the children had been given to her
charge, and that she had left them. All other pain
was less than that pain, the thought that they would
have been safe if she had never trusted them alone.

The day wore on, and the dim light began to
grow dimmer. When the twilight had almost come,
light flakes of snow began to fall like soft white
feathers through the trees. Then Lizzy burst out into
louder crying, and Barbara sank down upon the
ground and took both the little ones into her arms.
The child—such a mere child she was still in years,
and yet in heart so womanly and tender—pressed the
other little faces on her breast and held them there.
It was all that she could do. She herself sat blankly
looking at the snow as it came down, flake after flake,
soft and white and silent, till all hope left her, and in

those moments perhaps at last the little heart broke. "O mother! mother!" was the only thing she said.

Once more, after a few moments, she tried to make Lizzy rise up, that they might go on again, but the child, when she roused her, burst into weary, passionate sobs.

"I can't! I'm so tired! I can't go on!" she said; and then Davie awoke and began to moan too.

"O, I want to get home! When shall we get home? I'm so cold!" he sobbed.

She had a little brown cloth cloak on, and she took it off and wrapped it round the child. Twice more, as it got darker,—with a last forlorn effort,—she rose up again and carried the children on a little farther, the snow falling still over them, but yet falling gently, seeming to touch them almost tenderly, as if it was sorry for the little lost wanderers; then at last the end of the weary struggle came. She could do no more. She sat down with them at the foot of a great tree. "Perhaps somebody will come in the morning, and find us, and take us home," she said.

There were dead leaves on the ground, and she gathered them together as well as she could in the darkness, and made the children lie down upon them side by side. They were moaning and crying with hunger and cold. She rubbed their little limbs till they were warm, and took off their shoes and stockings, and warmed their feet upon her breast. She had already taken off her cloak for Davie; now, as they still went on crying, one by one she stripped herself of her other clothes, and wrapped the little ones up in them. Then she lay down beside them, and took them both as she best could in her arms.

The boy was frightened and restless. "Try to go to sleep, Davie," she said to him. "If mother was here she would like you to go to sleep." And then presently she remembered a little hymn that he was fond of, and sang it to him.

That was the last thing that either of the little ones heard her do. Warmed by the clothes that she had robbed herself of to give them, and by each other's arms and hers, they fell asleep while she was still singing.

My story has a half-sad ending, but I think you guess it already, and I need hardly tell it to you. I think there were angels looking down on Barbara as she sang that hymn, and that their arms were very near her when in the cold night the beating of her little heart grew faint. When morning came, those who had been looking for the children found them, and David and Lizzy woke up—still warm and breathing—from their sleep; but in the cottage on the hillside there is one empty seat now, and one little pair of feet the fewer is on the floor, and the mother has lost something that she will never find again on earth. Good bye to little Barbara! Think of her tenderly, but do not pity her; those who live to do what Barbara did, want no pity from one of *us*.

THE END.

PRINTING OFFICE OF THE PUBLISHER.

August 1890.

Tauchnitz Edition.

Latest Volumes:

Blind Love. By Wilkie Collins, 2 vols.
The Heritage of Dedlow Marsh, etc. By Bret Harte, 1 v.
A Life's Remorse. By the Author of "Molly Bawn," 2 v.
Allan's Wife and other Tales. By H. Rider Haggard, 1 v.
The New Prince Fortunatus. By William Black, 2 vols.
A History of the Four Georges. By Justin McCarthy, vol. 2.
A Yankee at the Court of King Arthur. By Mark Twain, 2 v.
Under Salisbury Spire. By Emma Marshall, 1 vol.
A Waif of the Plains. By Bret Harte, 1 vol.
Syrlin. By Ouida, 3 vols.
The Black-Box Murder, 1 vol.
A Daughter's Sacrifice. By F. C. Philips and P. Fendall, 1 v.
The Bondman. By Hall Caine, 2 vols.
Plain Tales from the Hills. By Rudyard Kipling, 1 vol.
The Sin of Joost Avelingh. By Maarten Maartens, 1 vol.
Donovan. By Edna Lyall, 2 vols.
In Thoughtland and in Dreamland. By Elsa D'Esterre-
    Keeling, 1 vol.
The Rajah's Heir, 2 vols.
Beatrice. By H. Rider Haggard, 2 vols.
The Duke's Daughter. By Mrs. Oliphant, 1 vol.
The Burnt Million. By James Payn, 2 vols.
A Reputed Changeling. By Charlotte M. Yonge, 2 vols.
Blindfold. By Florence Marryat, 2 vols.
The House of the Wolf. By Stanley J. Weyman, 1 vol.
For Faith and Freedom. By Walter Besant, 2 vols.

Joshua. By Georg Ebers. From the German by Clara and
    Margaret Bell, 2 vols. (*German Authors.*)

A complete Catalogue of the Tauchnitz
Edition is attached to this work.